Heartland

Every New Day

Heartland

❧

Share every moment . . .

Coming Home

After the Storm

Breaking Free

Taking Chances

Come What May

One Day You'll Know

Out of the Darkness

Thicker Than Water

Every New Day

Heartland

❧

Every New Day

by Lauren Brooke

SCHOLASTIC INC.

New York Toronto London Auckland Sydney
Mexico City New Delhi Hong Kong Buenos Aires

No part of this publication may be reproduced in whole or in part, or stored in a retrieval system, or transmitted in any form or by any means, electronic, mechanical, photocopying, recording, or otherwise, without written permission of the publisher. For information regarding permission, write to Scholastic Inc., Attention: Permissions Department, 557 Broadway, New York, NY 10012.

Library of Congress Cataloging-in-Publication data available.

ISBN 0-439-31716-9

Heartland series created by Working Partners Ltd, London.

Copyright © 2002 by Working Partners Ltd.
Published by Scholastic Inc. All rights reserved.

SCHOLASTIC and associated logos are trademarks and/or registered trademarks of Scholastic Inc. HEARTLAND is a trademark and/or registered trademark of Working Partners Ltd.

12 11 10 9 8 7 6 5 4 3   2 3 4 5 6 7/0
Printed in the U.S.A.   40
First Scholastic printing, September 2002

With special thanks to Gill Harvey

*For Kevin Yates — a good friend to Heartland
and to me*

Chapter One

The horse surged forward, his long white tail streaming behind him. Amy watched breathlessly as his hooves thundered over the ground. His rider sat effortlessly, seemingly a part of the horse's back, and the horse moved from a canter to a gallop. After a dozen fluid strides he slowed smoothly to a canter once more, then a trot.

The horse raised his head proudly. He was magnificent. The man on his back looked serene. While no reins connected horse and rider and no saddle sat between them, the respect they shared for each other was clear to see. It looked like the most natural, most intimate relationship.

Amy was moved. Although she knew so much about the special bond that can exist between horses and humans, she had never seen anything quite as powerful as this. The horse was responding freely to the tiniest shifts in the Native American's weight. She smiled as the pair approached the gate of the training ring where she stood watching. The old man's features barely moved, but she saw a glimmer of warmth in his eyes as he slipped lightly off the horse's back.

"Hi, I'm Amy Fleming," she said. "You must be Huten."

The man gave her a steady glance of appraisal as he began to unlatch the gate.

"Your son, Bill, sent me down from the house," Amy explained. "I'm visiting the area with my sister. You knew my mother — Marion Fleming, from Heartland Farm in Virginia. We came by to return a book you lent her."

Recognition sprang into the old man's eyes.

"Marion Fleming," he murmured. "The one with the magic touch." Then his dark eyes narrowed as he realized what Amy had said. "Knew?" he queried, searching Amy's face.

"Yes," said Amy quietly. "She — she died last year." Even though Amy had come to terms with losing her mother, telling people about it still caused a wave of grief to wash over her.

A veil of sadness seemed to fall on Huten's face. Then he turned to Amy and looked at her more closely. "You've been here before," he said softly. "I remember your face."

Amy nodded, astonished that he could remember her. "Yes," she said. "I came here with my mom. But I was only six."

She couldn't remember the details of the trip that she and Marion had made to Ocanumba, this area high in the Appalachian Mountains — it had been nine years ago. But some things had stuck in her mind. She remembered a lot of warmth and laughter and the sense of belonging to a big, happy family while she was there.

Huten and the paint horse came out of the schooling ring. The horse followed closely behind the man, still without a halter or lead rope to guide him. They all walked up a shaded dirt path, with the mountain rising up on one side.

"It was amazing, watching you ride," said Amy. "The way you work is really special."

The old man smiled slowly. "It's Albatross who's special," he said, reaching up to stroke the horse's neck. "They said he was a rogue horse, but he's not like that at all. He just knows his own mind. And he doesn't have much respect for most people."

"Mom always said there was no such thing as a rogue horse," said Amy.

"And she was right," agreed Huten. "Most horses don't need to be forced to do things. But if a horse doesn't want to do something, it usually has a pretty good reason."

Amy nodded. That was another one of the principles that her mom had taught her. But Amy hadn't seen many horses as responsive as Albatross, who was willing to be guided without a bridle or saddle. Albatross snorted as he walked along beside them and shook his head to chase away flies. Amy helped to swat them away, then scratched his neck. He must be a very special horse, true, but she suspected that his trust had a lot to do with the way that Huten had approached him and how the two had bonded.

✤

Amy's sister was standing at the top of the path waiting for them, her short blond hair gleaming in the sun.

"That's my sister, Lou," Amy said to Huten. "She went for a walk in the woods while I came to find you."

"She wasn't with you when you visited with your mother," commented Huten.

Again, Amy was impressed by his memory. "No," she said. "Lou grew up in England. She's only lived in the States since she finished college."

They reached Lou, and Amy smiled. "Lou, this is Huten Whitepath," she said.

Lou held out her hand. "Delighted to meet you." She smiled.

Huten nodded and held out his hand, giving a small

smile in return. "Please go on up to the cabin," he said. "I'll just take Albatross to his stall."

Amy and Lou walked up the path to a big wooden cabin nestled between ten majestic beech trees.

"Lou, it was amazing watching him," Amy said to her sister in a low voice. "I wish you'd seen it. Huten just has this incredible bond with Albatross. It's like they can read each other's mind. No wonder Mom liked being here."

Lou smiled. "Well, I had a great walk in the woods," she said. "This place is so peaceful. It's nice to get away, isn't it?"

Amy nodded, breathing in the crisp spring air. Ocanumba was surrounded by forest for miles around. As they neared the cabin, a Native American woman came out to meet them.

"Hi," she greeted them with a firm handshake and easy smile. "I'm Barbara, Bill's wife. He told me you'd dropped by to visit Huten. Come in, come in."

They followed her into the cabin. It was spacious but cozy, with beautiful textiles hanging from the walls. Barbara ushered them through the main room to the kitchen, which had a wood-burning stove and a long table at one end.

"We spend almost all our time in here," said Barbara. "It's the warmest place in the house. Our winters are no joke, as you can imagine." She popped her head around the kitchen door and called into the next room. "Carey, come and say hi."

A moment later, a girl a couple of years older than Amy came into the kitchen. Amy was struck by how much she looked like Huten. She had a small, wiry frame and her grandfather's striking black eyebrows, but it was more than that. She had the same quiet confidence and careful reserve in the way she looked at people.

"Hi, I'm Amy Fleming."

"And I'm Lou."

"Hi," said Carey somewhat abruptly.

Amy looked at her curiously. The family resemblance was strong, but Carey seemed to lack Huten's openness, as though she didn't want to get into any casual chitchat with visitors.

"Sit yourselves down," said Barbara. "Bill and Huten will come in a minute. I made a pecan pie this morning that needs eating. I'm glad you stopped by."

Bill and Huten came in just as she finished speaking, and in minutes a pot of steaming coffee was sitting on the table.

"You're just here for a few days, then?" Bill smiled as Barbara served up slices of the pie. Unlike Huten and Carey, Bill was chatty and jovial — *just like Barbara*, thought Amy.

"Less," said Lou regretfully. "Just for the weekend. We got here on Friday night, and we're heading back tomorrow morning. We can't really be away from Heartland for any more than two nights."

"What's Heartland?" asked Carey.

"It's the farm where we live," explained Amy. "It belongs to our Grandpa, Jack Bartlett. He raised cattle there for years. When he retired, my mom turned it into a stable for horses that need help — if they've been abused or abandoned."

Huten regarded Amy with his thoughtful eyes. "Now that Marion's gone, who is doing the rescue work?" he asked. At these words, Amy noticed Carey, Bill, and Barbara turn to look at her in surprise.

But it was Lou who answered. "Amy is," she said, adopting her businesslike tone. "With one of the stable hands, Ty. They've been able to adopt Mom's practices. Heartland still has the same mission as when Mom started out."

"We use lots of different remedies, depending on what the problem is," added Amy. "But the important thing is that we always listen to the horse, like you do here."

Huten nodded slowly and seemed to drift off into thoughts of his own.

"So how big is the stable?" asked Bill.

"We have eighteen stalls," said Amy. "But I guess we only have sixteen or seventeen horses on average. As soon as a horse is cured, we try to find it a new home and then give its place to another horse in need. That's how it works."

"Don't you go to school?" Carey questioned Amy curiously.

"Of course," said Amy, smiling. "But I get up at six every morning to help with the morning feeds and mucking out, then I work with the horses when I get home."

Carey raised an eyebrow. "You must get exhausted," she commented.

Amy found that Carey's tone put her on the defensive. "Yeah, but I love it," she said passionately. Yet she felt confused. Why was Carey critical of her devotion to the horses? Why wouldn't she feel the same way, having someone like Huten as her grandfather?

                                ❧

Huten suddenly came out of his reverie and leaned forward in his chair. He searched Amy's face with his dark eyes. "How well do you remember your visit here, Amy?" he asked her.

Amy thought back. "Not very well," she admitted. "I don't think we were here very long. But I remember that Mom seemed really happy."

She exchanged glances with Lou. Nine years ago, their mother had still been coming to terms with the fact that her husband, Tim, had left her. He had been an

Olympic show jumper, but after being seriously injured in a terrible accident, he had deserted the family without a word.

Huten nodded. "Yes. She was happy because she was finding her true self — her healing touch."

Amy listened. It was weird, meeting a stranger who understood what her mom had been through.

"And in her newfound happiness," continued Huten, "she made a promise — a promise that she never kept."

"What kind of promise?" Amy asked, feeling anxious. She hated hearing anything negative about her mom.

"She said she'd come back," said Huten. "She said she'd bring one of her horses for us to work on together." He paused. "She said she'd know when the right time had come, and then she'd find me."

Amy shot Lou another glance. Over the last few months, they had discovered many things about Marion that they hadn't known before.

"But she never came back," Huten carried on. "That right time never came, and now her time has gone."

Amy took a deep breath. "Heartland was always really busy," she said. "I guess . . ." she trailed off.

Huten smiled slowly. "I know. I understand," he said. "The right time has a habit of hiding itself. It always lies just out of our view."

A silence fell around the table. Amy pondered Huten's words and avoided Lou's gaze. She could sense that her sister was feeling a bit uncomfortable. Amy herself felt that what he was saying was slightly strange. It was as though, in some way, Huten knew more about their mother than she and Lou knew themselves. And now it sounded like he felt offended, having been cheated of her promise. She didn't know what to say.

The Whitepath family seemed at home with the silence, and Bill asked for another piece of pie.

"We brought back your book," said Amy eventually.

Huten nodded. "I know the one," he said. "*Hearing the Silence.*"

Amy nodded. She reached down into her bag and fished out a small hardback book. The cover was blue and faded at the edges. "Here it is." She handed it to Huten. She hesitated, then said, "You wrote an inscription. '*When this book no longer holds any answers, the time is right.*' I think I know what you mean now."

"Thank you," he said quietly.

Amy hesitated. "I'm really sorry the right time never came."

❧

The afternoon light was lengthening the shadows of the trees as Lou and Amy left the cabin.

"I'll show you around the rest of the yard," offered Bill. "If you have time."

"That would be great," Amy said enthusiastically, relieved to have a distraction.

She and Lou followed him down the path.

"There are quite a few stables in the area," said Bill.
"Plenty of people who come here on vacation like to ride
into the hills. But we don't do too much work with
tourists here at Ten Beeches. Huten and I work more
with problem horses."

"Just like we do at Heartland," said Amy.

"I guess that's why your mom brought you here," said
Bill, smiling at Amy. He led them around the stalls,
where horses were pulling at their hay nets.

"You know, although we're supposed to be working
with horses, we do almost as much work with people,"
Bill went on. "People get drawn to Ocanumba. They
seem to find answers here. This land has a serene qual-
ity, a real history, I guess because the Native Americans
feel a true connection with their space. We cherish our
old ways and work to keep our heritage alive."

Amy thought about Bill's words as they wandered
along the stalls. Much of what he was saying applied to
Heartland as well. She thought of the peacefulness of
their land, nestled in the hills. She stopped at the stall of
a rough-coated pony. He looked tough, and Amy guessed
he had some mustang blood. Despite his shagginess, Amy
could tell that he was too thin. As she held out her hand,

he flinched and retreated to the back of his stall, eyeing her nervously.

"He looks lost," said Amy softly, her heart reaching out to the frightened animal.

"That's Maverick," said Bill. "He's had a bad time. He was so malnourished when he came to us. Getting him back into any kind of shape has been a long haul. And he's half wild, too. Gentling him is sure taking time."

Amy longed to enter the stall. There was something about the pony that drew her to him. But Lou was obviously beginning to be concerned about the time.

"Amy, we should really get going," said Lou. "It's getting late, and we still have a long drive to the motel."

"OK," Amy said reluctantly. "I guess we should go back and say good-bye to everyone."

They walked back to the cabin, and Amy saw the first stars beginning to show themselves in the sky above the darkness of the mountain. She sighed. This place really was perfect.

"It's a shame we can't stay longer," she said to Lou in a low voice.

Lou smiled. "Not missing Heartland?" she asked in a teasing voice. "Or anyone at Heartland?"

Amy smiled gently. Lou was talking about Ty and Amy's relationship, which still seemed very strange and new to Amy, especially after they'd been friends for so long.

"Well . . ." said Amy. "I guess it'll be good to get back."

❧

"The right time has a habit of hiding itself," Amy mused the next morning as they sped along the road back toward Heartland in Lou's car. "What do you think Huten meant by that? Why do you think Mom never went back?"

Lou hesitated. "I'm not so sure Mom wanted to go back," she said.

"Why not?" asked Amy. She remembered how uncomfortable Lou had seemed during the conversation.

"Well, Heartland's always been busy and bringing a horse all this way is a crazy idea. She probably just made some throwaway comment about going back there sometime. I'm sure she meant to be sincere, but he made it seem like she'd sort of let herself down. Or let him down. I don't know why he took it so seriously."

Amy frowned. She didn't see it that way at all. She knew that Marion would have done anything for a horse if she thought it would help. She wouldn't have let a drive to the Appalachians get in her way. Besides, she believed her mom's time at Ocanumba had been special and that she would have wanted to return.

But Amy knew she and Lou had different ways of looking at things. They'd both found it difficult to adjust to all the changes since their mother's death. Lou had moved back to Heartland from her banking job in

Manhattan to look after the business side of things. Then, in an attempt to rebuild their family, Lou had tracked down their father, Tim. They'd finally been able to meet with him three weeks ago, when he'd been on a business trip to the States.

Tim's visit hadn't been easy. Lou hadn't connected with him at all, while Amy discovered they shared an unexpected bond. It was hard for both sisters to deal with all the tides of emotion, which was why their grandfather had suggested that Lou and Amy go away for a weekend together. It had seemed like an odd idea at first. Then Amy had come across *Hearing the Silence* in Marion's old bedroom and had suggested they visit Ocanumba to return it.

Amy sighed, thinking about what Lou had said. "I don't think Huten meant that Mom had let anyone down," she said slowly. "I got the feeling that he had a real connection with Mom and that he was sad, knowing he'd never see her again. I just think he was saying that it can be difficult to recognize the right time to do something, to make the time. And now it's too late."

Lou shrugged. "I'm not so sure," she said cautiously. "Anyway, most things come down to what's possible, at the end of the day. You know, what's practical."

"Practical?" teased Amy. "That's you all over, Lou!"

Lou flushed slightly, but she smiled, too. "Well, some-

one has to be realistic around here," she said. Amy
grinned at her sister and stared out the window.

Maybe Lou was right. Maybe it wasn't a good idea,
thinking that Marion had missed her chance to go back
and visit Huten. Either things happened or they didn't.
But Amy felt there was something special about the way
that Huten looked at things — something that had clearly
affected Marion, all those years ago. Maybe if Lou had
seen him riding Albatross, she'd have felt it, too.

"I thought we'd drop by Safeway on the way home,"
said Lou. "Saves another trip later. Are you in a rush to
get back?"

"No, that's OK," said Amy. "We might as well go
now."

They were on the outskirts of their town. Lou turned
off the highway and into the Safeway parking lot.

"Lou!" exclaimed Amy as Lou pulled into a parking
space. "There's Ty!"

Sure enough, Ty's tall figure was striding purposefully
toward the store entrance. "I'll run and catch up with
him," said Amy with a grin. "Do you need me to stick
around, or can I get a ride back with him?"

"No, sure," said Lou, smiling at Amy's obvious display
of excitement. "I'll see you back at Heartland."

Amy got out of Lou's car and sprinted toward the supermarket entrance. Inside, Ty had disappeared into the crowd of shoppers. She hunted for him up and down the aisles.

"Ty!" she called, suddenly spotting him.

Ty whirled around in surprise. "Amy!" he exclaimed as she walked up to him. "I missed you! What are you doing here?"

Then before she could answer, he hugged her impulsively. Amy was taken by surprise and looked up at him, laughing. He grinned and leaned down to give her a kiss.

"Ty!" she protested, ducking away. "We're in the grocery store!"

"So? What's the big deal?" asked Ty.

"That's a good question, Amy," came a voice from behind them. Amy turned around in horror. Ashley Grant — of all people.

Ashley tossed her perfectly trimmed blond hair over her shoulder and gave Amy a triumphant grin. "So, there's romance budding under the detergent," she said. "What a nice surprise. You haven't been trying to keep this a secret, have you?"

Amy stared at her, her face hot. Ashley was the last person in the world she would have told about dating Ty. Ashley was in Amy's class at school and had a nasty habit of being catty about everything. Especially things involving Amy.

"But I have to agree with Ty. There's no better place to announce an affair than a supermarket." A smug smile reached across Ashley's face.

"It's none of your business, Ashley," she said coldly.

"Of course not, Amy," Ashley replied. "But talking of business, it's not really professional to be dating your stable hand, is it? Not that I'm surprised, with Heartland being such a low-class establishment."

Amy felt rage rising in her throat. As if Ashley knew anything about how to treat horses — or people, for that matter! Her mother, Val, ran a high-scale stable called Green Briar that specialized in training robotic little show ponies. She believed in firm discipline and bending horses to her will, not treating any horse as an individual. Green Briar went against everything that Heartland stood for. Amy opened her mouth for a sharp retort, but Ty took her firmly by the elbow.

"Come on," Ty said in a low voice. "She's not worth it. She's really not."

Amy swallowed her words and turned her back.

"Have a lovely day," Ashley called as Amy and Ty made their way up the supermarket aisle. "I'm sure you will."

Chapter Two

"Nice job, Mercury." Amy encouraged the gray gelding that trotted around her in a smooth circle. His neck was arched and he was moving beautifully. "That's a good boy," Amy murmured. She brought him to a halt and he responded willingly, standing square as she walked up to him and unclipped the longline.

"On your own, now," she said to him, moving back into the center of the schooling ring, coiling the longline around her arm. "Trot on!" she commanded. Obediently, Mercury moved forward into an energetic trot.

Amy watched the gelding intently as he moved around the ring. Mercury was a young show jumper that had arrived at Heartland a week ago. There was something about his movement that reminded Amy of Huten's session with Albatross the day before. Like

Albatross, he was responding freely and well, gracefully trotting around the ring with undeniable spirit, responding to her commands. *If only that was all he needed to do*, thought Amy. But his problems lay elsewhere.

Mercury's owners were two established trainers named Gabriel Adams and Bruce Haslam. They had spotted him as a talented youngster at a number of shows. They'd followed his progress and were surprised when he seemed to lose form — his jump had lost its spark. Then, about a year later, they saw an ad that he was for sale and went to see him. Mercury's jump was still off, but they thought they had quickly discovered what the problem was. The previous owners openly told Gabriel that they'd been rapping him — forcing him to jump higher by rapping his legs with a pole each time he jumped a fence.

Gabriel and Bruce had bought him, thinking they could quickly undo the damage. But Mercury didn't want to jump anymore. He refused even the smallest fences. Nothing they did seemed to help, so they'd brought him to Heartland.

"Turn!" Amy called in a firm voice. Neatly, Mercury spun around on his hind legs and trotted around the ring in the opposite direction. Amy studied his movement. There was no doubt that Mercury could still jump, if he wanted to. He was in perfect health, and his coat gleamed in the late afternoon sun. More than that, his whole body was springy and muscular — he had the perfect compact conformation of a jumper.

Amy spotted Ty watching over the fence and commanded Mercury to halt again. She walked over and took hold of his halter to lead him over to the fence. She smiled slightly awkwardly at Ty, still feeling embarrassed over the incident in the supermarket. But she really wanted to discuss Mercury with him.

"How's he doing?" asked Ty. "He seems to be going well."

"He is," agreed Amy. "I think the key is going to be taking him back to basics — taking him over simple trotting poles on the ground first. If we can get him to relax and realize that no one's going to rap him, maybe he'll gradually start to enjoy jumping again."

"Makes sense," Ty agreed. "Should I get some poles out for you?"

"Yeah, thanks," said Amy. "I'll keep working him at the top of the ring while you set them out."

Quickly, Ty moved poles from the edge of the ring into a neatly spaced-out line, each a stride apart. The gelding wouldn't even have to jump — all he had to do was pick up his feet slightly as he trotted over the poles.

"OK, ready when you are," he called to Amy as he finished.

Amy brought Mercury down to the bottom of the

school and attached the longline to his halter once more. Then she sent him off again, this time in a circle that would take him over the trotting poles.

As he reached the first pole, the gelding instantly stiffened. His head shot into the air, and he shied away violently.

"Trot on!" Amy called, keeping her voice calm. The gelding obeyed — but not by trotting over the poles. He carefully made his way around them, eyeing them nervously. He looked very different from the collected, responsive horse he'd been five minutes earlier.

Amy let him continue his circle until he came to the poles again.

"Come on, boy," she said to encourage him. But again, the gelding shied around them.

"He's determined not to do it," Amy said to Ty. She moved Mercury away from the poles and trotted him around until he was relaxed again. Then she brought him to a halt. She walked up to the gelding and patted his neck. It was still lathered and sweaty, but he had calmed down again. She walked him back over to Ty.

"I think we just have to take it really slowly," she said. "He's incredibly responsive otherwise — the rapping must have had a really big effect. It like he's traumatized."

Ty nodded, looking at Mercury's big, intelligent eyes and pricked ears. His delicate nostrils flared in and out quickly, showing his sensitive nature. "He's a lot like Red," he commented.

"Hey! That's exactly what I was thinking!" said Amy. Red belonged to Ben, the other stable hand, and was a talented young jumper. "Their temperaments are really similar." She paused as a thought occurred to her. "You know, Ty, maybe we should have Ben help more with Mercury. He's been here for almost six months, and he hasn't worked that much. I mean, he's been doing all the stable yard-work, but he hasn't been treating the horses, which is what he's here to learn about."

"And he understands Red inside and out," mused Ty. "I think that's a really good idea. He'll probably understand Mercury better than either of us."

Amy grinned. She and Ty usually thought the same way when it came to treating the horses.

"I'll talk to him about it later," said Amy. "In the meantime, I think we have to just keep on trying to gain Mercury's trust."

❧

As they walked Mercury up to the barns, Amy spotted Scott Trewin in the stable yard. Scott was the local equine vet — and he was Lou's boyfriend. Even from this distance, Amy could see that he had a broad smile on his face as she and Ty approached. She raised a hand in greeting, and he waved back.

"Scott's looking awfully happy about something!" she said to Ty. "Did anything happen when Lou and I were away?"

"Nothing," said Ty. "Well, not as far as I know."

They came within earshot. "Well, you guys sure have been keeping things quiet," Scott called.

Amy had no idea what he was talking about. She looked quickly at Ty. Then the realization dawned on her. Ashley! Scott's brother, Matt, was her boyfriend. Ashley must have told him about seeing them in the supermarket. But that had been only a few hours ago.

She felt a wave of embarrassment wash over her. How could Ashley just go blabbing to everyone like that? To her surprise, Ty was grinning. She shook her head in disbelief and then looked at Ty.

"Well, I guess news travels fast," he said with a light laugh.

"What's the news?" asked Ben as he came out of one of the front stalls.

Ty put his arm around Amy's shoulder. "Well," he said, "I guess we should have told you sooner, but —"

"Are you dating?" Ben asked in astonishment. "I wouldn't have known, but it makes sense. Congratulations!" Ben said, slapping Ty on the shoulder.

Amy blushed. She felt confused. She hadn't wanted everyone to know just yet. And if people were going to find out, she wanted to tell them herself.

Mercury tossed his head up and she patted his neck. "I'll just put Mercury in his stall," she said quickly, avoiding everyone's gaze. "He's getting restless."

She headed to his stall on the front yard, leaving Ty with Scott and Ben. Mercury nuzzled her hair as she undid the buckles on his bridle slowly, taking her time. She was thinking fast. So now nearly everyone knew about her and Ty. Lou had guessed that something was going on and it hadn't taken long for Amy's best friend, Soraya, to work it out, too. And now everyone at school would know because Ashley was obviously spreading the news around like some amateur reporter.

A shadow fell across the stall door and she looked up. It was Ty.

"Hey," he said. "Are you OK?"

"Fine," she said a bit abruptly as he let himself into the stall. She lifted the bridle over Mercury's ears and slung it over her shoulder.

"You don't . . . seem fine," said Ty cautiously. "Is something wrong?"

Amy sighed. "I just wish Ashley had kept her mouth shut, that's all," she said. "Now everyone knows. So we'll have to tell Grandpa — before someone else does."

"Well, that's OK, isn't it?" asked Ty. "We have to tell him sometime."

Amy hesitated. She wasn't really worried about Grandpa's reaction. He liked Ty, so he wouldn't have any serious objections. So what was it that was bothering her?

"I don't know," she muttered. "It would just have been easier to keep it quiet for a little while longer."

Ty stroked Mercury's neck thoughtfully. "We can't keep it a secret forever, Amy," he said softly. He reached out and touched her arm. "And anyway — I hoped you wouldn't want to."

Amy looked at him, searching his face. She could see the hurt there and confusion. "No. I know. I know," she said awkwardly. She smiled. "I'll tell Grandpa tonight."

❧

"Hey, Grandpa," Amy said later that night. "Did you have a good time?"

Jack Bartlett had been out visiting friends, and Lou had gone out with Scott. So Amy had spent the evening by herself, unpacking her bag from the weekend and watching TV.

"Yes, thanks," said Grandpa. He smiled. "But it's good to see you back. How was Ocanumba? Did you and Lou enjoy yourselves?"

"It was fantastic," said Amy. "We had a great time. And Huten was amazing. I watched his session with a paint horse. The bond they had was something else — unbelievable. I can see why Mom loved it there."

Jack Bartlett nodded thoughtfully. "I remember that

trip really helped her adjust to being back here in the States," he said. "I think it made her realize she was doing the right thing. When she got back, she became completely devoted to Heartland."

"I can understand that," said Amy. She knew that Marion's decision to return to Virginia hadn't been an easy one. It had meant admitting that her marriage with Tim was over and that he wasn't going to come back to her. But Ocanumba, and Ten Beeches in particular, was the sort of place that could reassure anyone.

"Did she talk about it much?" she asked Grandpa.

He frowned thoughtfully. "She talked about Huten's work, but I don't remember many of the details," he said. "She was just much more settled afterward. More at peace with herself."

Grandpa took off his shoes and flopped back into an armchair.

Amy absentmindedly studied her hands, realizing that the moment had come to tell him about Ty.

"Grandpa . . ." She hesitated, then spoke in a rush. "I've got to talk to you. I wanted to tell you with Ty here, but he's not around tonight, and I kind of want to tell you now."

Grandpa leaned forward at Amy's serious tone. "What is it?" he asked.

"It's me and — Ty," she answered.

"And . . . ?" probed Grandpa gently.

"Well — we've kind of started dating," finished Amy, looking up to meet his gaze.

Grandpa gave Amy a warm smile. "And I suppose I'm the last to know?"

"Well . . . I didn't mean it to be like that," said Amy. "Grandpa, I don't want it to change anything. I mean, our work at Heartland or anything. Ty's always been such a good friend."

"And there's no reason why he shouldn't remain one," said Grandpa seriously.

Amy sighed in relief. "I'm glad that's how you feel," she said.

"Why wouldn't I?" asked Grandpa.

So now everyone knows, Amy thought to herself. *Well, everyone who matters.* It was the next day — a beautiful morning — but Amy was preoccupied as she filled the water buckets and distributed the morning feeds. How many people would come up to her at school, wanting to know about Ty? And how would Matt have taken the news? Only a few months ago, he'd wanted to go out with Amy, but now he seemed happy dating Ashley.

Amy banged a bucket down under the yard tap, feeling irritable. She hated the way everyone got so wound up about "relationships." If people thought she was going to go around obsessing about her boyfriend, they were wrong. There were more important things to do.

❦

"See you later, Ty!" she called as she rushed to catch the bus. As usual, she was running late and didn't have time to find him. She heard him call back from inside one of the stalls and made her way down the driveway.

"Hi! How was the weekend?" asked Soraya the minute Amy sat beside her on the bus. "How was Ocanumba?"

"Great," said Amy. "The people there are so cool! I'd love to go back sometime and actually get to ride in the hills. Maybe I could even work with Huten." She suddenly realized that this idea had been sitting at the back of her mind ever since the old man told her about Marion's promise. She explained to Soraya what he'd said.

"Wow, that's pretty weird. I wonder why your mom never went back," said Soraya.

"I don't know," said Amy. "It's strange, because I got the feeling that she and Huten worked well together. I really don't remember much about what she did when we were there. But he said she had a magic touch with horses. I think she would have liked to have gone back, but she never had the chance."

"Maybe," said Soraya, waving as Matt got onto the bus. Slowly, he walked up the aisle of the bus. He hesitated, looking as though he might sit farther back. But then he seemed to change his mind and swung into the seat in front of them.

"Hello," he said coolly.

"How's it going?" asked Soraya. "Good weekend?"

Amy wished she'd had time to tell Soraya what had happened yesterday in Safeway.

"Fine," said Matt. He gave Amy a sharp look. "I hear you had a good weekend, too, Amy," he added.

"It was OK," Amy responded awkwardly.

Soraya looked from Matt to Amy with a bewildered expression.

Amy blushed and decided to ignore the issue. Instead, she said, "Lou and I went up to Ocanumba in the Appalachians."

"That's not what I heard," said Matt. "I heard you were loitering in aisle ten of Safeway."

Amy sucked in her breath sharply. She'd guessed that Matt might not react well, but she hadn't expected him to be so direct about it.

"So you saw Ashley over the weekend, then," she said as calmly as she could.

Matt just stared at her. "I thought you weren't into dating friends, Amy," he said.

Amy's blush deepened. When Matt had asked her out that was exactly what she'd said. She didn't know what to say now. "Well, I guess I was wrong," she said eventually.

Matt shrugged and turned away. Soraya raised an eyebrow. The three traveled in silence until they reached school.

"What was all that about?" whispered Soraya as soon as she had a chance. "I've never seen him so mad."

Amy gave her friend a wry smile. "I'll give you three guesses who saw Ty kissing me yesterday," she said.

A puzzled look crossed over Soraya's face. Her eyes widened with disbelief as the truth dawned on her. "Not — Ashley?" she said.

"Yep," said Amy. "Got it in one."

❧

"Hey! Steady, Mercury," said Amy, soothing the gelding, who was spooking at the sight of Soraya riding into the yard on her bicycle. Soraya, Ben, and Amy had planned a ride on the trails after school, and Amy was just saddling Mercury.

"That's a boy," Amy said. "You need a good gallop on the trails, don't you?"

"He's gorgeous," Soraya enthused. "What's he here for?"

"He's a jumper," Amy explained. "But he's refusing to jump because his first owners rapped him really badly."

"So are you getting anywhere with him?" Soraya asked.

"Not yet," admitted Amy. "I'm going to get Ben to help. Mercury and Red have really similar temperaments."

As she spoke, Ben brought Red from the barn, tacked up and ready to go. He gave Soraya a big grin. "Hi," he greeted her. "Who are you riding?"

"I thought you could ride Sovereign," Amy answered for her. "We're still working on his fear of traffic, but we won't be going near any roads. I've already tacked him up. He's in his stall."

"Great," said Soraya. "I'll go and get him."

Soon the three were making their way up the trail that led between the trees to Clairdale Ridge. Mercury danced, itching to be given his head.

"He's totally full of energy," Amy said. She eased him forward into a trot, and they rode along in single file up the path for a while. When the trail opened out a little, they slowed to a walk and rode alongside one another. Mercury and Red arched their necks and competed, each trying to take the lead. Mercury tossed his head, trying to snatch the reins from Amy's grip.

"They're a real pair," laughed Soraya. "I've never seen

two horses challenge each other that way." Sovereign wasn't joining in with the competition; he was quite happy to walk sedately behind the other two.

"Yeah," agreed Amy. "In fact that's something I wanted to talk to you about, Ben. I've been discussing Mercury's treatment with Ty. We think it would be a good idea for you to work with him, if you want to get more involved. What do you think?"

Ben's face lit up. "That'd be great!" he exclaimed. "Mercury's my kind of horse. It would be fantastic to get him jumping again."

Amy grinned. "I thought you'd feel that way," she said. "We're taking him back to basics for now, working with him on the flat with trotting poles. We're hoping that if we build his trust and make him realize we're not going to rap him, he'll start enjoying jumping again."

Ben nodded. "That makes sense," he said. "Well, I'll be glad to help."

They reached a broad, flat field, and Ben eased Red forward into a canter. Red gave a playful buck as he set off. Amy held Mercury back a second, then let him follow a few strides behind. Soraya brought up the rear, and the three horses stretched their stride out to a gallop. Amy laughed with exhilaration. Mercury's stride was full of energy, and he was soon alongside Red. Then he passed him and raced ahead.

At the end of the field, a few dry logs spread across the

continuation of the trail. Amy pulled Mercury up, knowing that Ben would want to take Red over the logs. Ben rode Red in a circle to calm him down after the gallop. Then, before turning Red toward the logs, he trotted over to Amy.

"Amy, I have an idea," said Ben. "About Mercury. If he's anything like Red, now's the time to get him jumping. He's all fired up after the gallop, and the logs are really simple and inviting. And he's been competing with Red, so if Red jumps the logs first he's bound to follow."

Amy hesitated. She and Ty knew how important it was to take things slowly and not undo any good work they'd done. But everything Ben said was true — and she was still having difficulty holding Mercury. The gallop hadn't used up all his energy by a long shot. Any spirited horse was likely to love the opportunity to go over the logs, which weren't high at all.

"Well — OK," she said. "It's worth a try. Take Red over the logs first, and I'll follow a few strides behind."

Ben grinned and rode Red in another circle. Amy trotted Mercury in a wide circle as well, then let him watch as Ben turned Red toward the logs. Gently, she urged Mercury forward into a canter to follow him. Red sailed over the logs with ease, and Amy patted Mercury's neck. "Come on, boy," she murmured. "You can do it that easily, too."

Mercury cantered steadily toward the logs. For a moment, Amy thought that Ben was right. Mercury was going to follow Red without even thinking about it. But then, at the last minute, it was as though he suddenly realized what Amy was asking him to do. He shied violently and veered around the logs, almost throwing Amy off his back.

Amy gasped. She lost a stirrup but managed to keep her seat. "Hey! Steady, boy," she soothed, but Mercury tossed his head and spun away from the logs.

"Hey, hey," said Amy, sitting deep in the saddle and asking him to drop his nose onto the bit. Mercury pranced on the spot, his nose in the air and his back hollowed. Amy couldn't get him to listen. And when a shrieking bird flew out from a nearby thicket, he shied again. Before Amy could react, he put his head down and bolted — away from Ben and Red and the logs.

"Amy!" cried Soraya's voice on the wind.

But all Amy could hear were Mercury's hooves eating up the ground, flying toward the narrow path at the other end of the field.

Chapter Three

Determined not to panic, Amy let Mercury gallop on, giving and taking with the reins to let him know that she was still there. Just as they reached the point where the trail narrowed, he slowed to an agitated canter.

Amy pulled him back to a trot, and he responded, his sides heaving. She brought him to a halt and jumped off, going quickly to his head to reassure him. His eyes were rolling, and he still looked distressed.

"Oh, Mercury," said Amy, realizing that her knees were shaking. "I'm sorry, boy. You're just not ready, are you?" She stroked his face and waited as Ben and Soraya cantered up slowly, looking anxious.

"Amy, are you OK?" asked Ben. His face was a mask of guilt. "I feel awful. I should never have suggested that you encourage Mercury to jump."

"I'm fine," Amy reassured him. "And it's not your fault. I thought it seemed like a good idea, too."

"Well," said Ben, "I'm still sorry. I guess I don't know that much about Mercury yet."

"Maybe not, but I thought it was worth a shot," said Amy. She stroked Mercury's neck. His breathing was steadier now. Lightly, Amy swung herself back into the saddle. She smiled reassuringly at Soraya, who still looked worried.

They turned the horses' heads back onto the trail to Heartland and walked on sedately, letting them cool down. Amy turned to Ben and said, "You know, a good way for you to get to know Mercury would be to lunge him while I'm at school. That way, you'll get a feel for what he's like."

"Are you sure I'm up to it?" Ben asked dubiously.

"Ben, it's just lunging. What just happened wasn't your fault," insisted Amy again. "You're great with horses. Of course you're up to it."

Ben gave a little smile. "OK. Thanks, Amy. I'd really like to work with him. I'll take it slow. I promise."

Back at the yard, Amy took Mercury to his stall to give him a thorough rubdown. His coat was still totally lathered from his headlong gallop, and his muscles were wired and tense. When she had finished rubbing him down, she began massaging his back in tiny T-touch circles with her fingers, then worked gradually up his neck, talking to him in a low voice. At the back of her mind was the thought that if she and Ty had made any progress at all with Mercury over the last week, it had all gone to waste.

To her relief, she began to feel Mercury relax as her fingers did their work.

"Are you OK, Amy?" asked Lou from the stall door. "Soraya told me what happened on the trail."

Amy looked up at Lou's worried face. "I'm fine, Lou," she said. "It's not the first time a horse has bolted with me. I guess it won't be the last, either."

Lou frowned anxiously, and Amy realized how difficult it was for her sister when something like this happened. She'd only realized just *how* difficult in the past few weeks, during their father's visit. Lou had admitted to him that she hadn't been able to ride since the day of his accident.

"Do you know why he bolted?" Lou asked, leaning on the stall door to watch Amy's expert fingers at work.

"He got scared," said Amy. "He just panicked and ran. He couldn't help himself." She hesitated, then added gently, "I wasn't in any real danger."

"No, I guess not," said Lou awkwardly. She paused, then said, "I was just about to groom Rosie. Would you show me how to do T-touch on her?"

Amy looked at her sister and smiled. Lou was obviously making a big effort to be more involved with the horses, even though she had a long way to go to overcome all her fears.

"Sure," she said with a grin. "I'll come and find you when I'm finished here."

Lou headed off in the direction of the tack room while Amy started to work on Mercury's face. Then she went over to Rosie's stall. Lou was already busy with a body brush, absorbed in her work.

"T-touch works really well with Rosie," said Amy, letting herself into the stall. "She loves it. I think it's helped a lot."

Rosie had arrived at the stable a few weeks earlier. She'd been badly head shy and hated anyone touching her head. To make matters worse, she'd hit her head and had sustained a slight fracture. But she was almost completely cured of both problems. Amy's T-touch work over the last few weeks had really helped. She was almost ready to go back to her owners.

Quickly, Amy showed Lou how to make light T-touch circles with her fingers, starting on the mare's back and working up toward her head. Lou watched intently, then took over.

"I'll leave you to it," said Amy.

"OK, Amy. Thanks," said Lou. She hesitated. "Sorry for worrying earlier," she added.

Amy smiled. "I'd already forgotten about it," she said. But as she left the stall, she wondered if Lou would ever really be at ease with horses again — if she would ever completely lose her fear.

❧

The following evening, Amy hunted down Ben as soon as she got home from school. He was in the feed room, starting work on the evening feeds.

"Hi, Ben!" Amy called. "Did you do a session with Mercury today?"

Ben gave her a grin. "Yeah," he said. "A really short one. He's great to work with on the lunge."

"He responds well, doesn't he?" said Amy. "Did he seem nervous after what happened yesterday?"

"No, he seemed pretty relaxed," Ben said. "But I didn't try him over any trotting poles or anything. We were only out for about twenty minutes."

"Oh, that's good," said Amy. She thought for a minute. "So he could probably do another session now. Do you want to come and help?"

"Sure," Ben said enthusiastically. "I'll just finish mixing these feeds."

"OK. See you down at the training ring," she called out, already making her way toward the stalls.

Amy decided to ride Mercury this time rather than lunging him again. She saddled him up and rode him down to the main training ring. As she began to trot around, she saw Ben come and perch himself on the fence.

Amy rode Mercury through his paces. Ben was right. He didn't seem to have reacted too badly to his scare the day before. Soon she rode him over to the fence and jumped off.

"Why don't you try riding him?" she suggested. "You're so used to Red. I bet Mercury will respond really well to you."

Ben looked pleased and quickly mounted. Amy watched carefully as the gelding trotted around the ring. Her instincts were right — Ben soon had Mercury going well, his powerful hindquarters pushing him forward into a full-length stride. As they broke into a canter, Ty came down from the stable yard and stood beside Amy.

"He's still going well," Ty commented as Ben and Mercury passed by.

"On the flat," agreed Amy. "I'm sure yesterday's experience won't have helped with his jumping problem, though. Anyway, I think it's good that Ben's involved with him now. We'll see how it goes."

They watched as Ben started working Mercury in some figure eights and serpentines, then some circles. As he asked Mercury to ride a tighter circle, Amy thought she noticed a sudden change in the gelding. Even from across the ring she could see he tensed up. Ben completed the circle and trotted him around the ring again. Then he asked Mercury to circle again. This time, he tensed immediately. Mercury's head came up, and he hollowed his back. He started to resist. It was clear that Ben could feel the difference, too. A puzzled frown of concentration came over his face, and he tried circling the gelding again, this time in the other direction.

Now Mercury was openly fighting. He tossed his head and tried to snatch at the reins. Ben pushed him on with his legs, not allowing him to get the upper hand.

Amy had a sudden thought.

"Ben!" she called, looking at Ty quickly. "He thinks you're going to make him jump."

Ty leaned into the fence. "It sure looks like it," he agreed.

"Go back to bigger circles," called Amy. "Or just take him around the outside ring."

Ben looked up, frustration on his face. "OK," he called back reluctantly. He returned to working around the full ring, and Mercury began to relax. When he was going well again, Ben brought him over to the fence.

"I'd never let Red get away with something like that," he said.

"I know," said Amy, "but Red's not damaged the way Mercury is." She explained her theory. "He reacts badly to anything associated with jumping. He's probably had enough for today. Let's finish now, while he's still going well."

Ben dismounted, and they made their way up to the yard. Ben was quiet, and Amy thought he looked disappointed with how the session had gone.

"Don't blame yourself, Ben," she said. "We've just hit upon one more thing that Mercury won't do. He doesn't want to face jumping, and it's not surprising."

She realized the truth of her own words as she spoke. Mercury really didn't want to have anything more to do with his painful past. And how could they make him want to? All of a sudden, the vision of Huten's calm face came into her mind, and she recalled his words as they walked up the path together. *Most horses don't need to be forced to do things. If they don't want to do something, they usually have a pretty good reason.* Well, it was obvious what Mercury's reasons were . . . so how could they move beyond them?

✣

"Ty?" Amy called softly, putting her head around the tack room door. They'd finished supper and the yard was quiet. She and Ty had hardly gotten a chance to see each other alone over the past few days.

"Yeah, I'm here," said Ty. He was sitting on one of the storage trunks at the back, reading a horse magazine. He put it down and smiled warmly as Amy came in. She was feeling a bit nervous. It still felt very odd, being more than friends. He reached out his arm and drew her to him. She pulled herself onto the trunk next to him.

"Good day?" he asked.

Amy put her head tentatively on his shoulder. "Much better now," she said. "How about you?"

"Fine," said Ty. "But it seemed really long. It just dragged on especially while you were at school. I feel like I hardly ever see you."

"Well — there was the session with Mercury," said Amy.

"That's work," said Ty. "You know what I mean. We don't see much of each other on our own."

Amy felt uncomfortable. Working with Ty was one of the things she loved best about being with him. She didn't want that to change.

"I guess," she said. "Well, I'm here now."

"All of you?" teased Ty.

Amy grinned. "Most of me," she said. "I think part of me is inside, studying for my history test, and another part is in Mercury's stall, trying to work out what's going on in his head."

Ty laughed. "Why am I not surprised to hear you say that — at least the part about Mercury?" he said. Then he looked thoughtful. "It's not going too well, is it?"

Amy sighed. "Not really. He's just perfect until you ask him to do anything that reminds him of jumping."

"And Ben helping out isn't really working, either," added Ty.

Amy looked at him quickly.

"What do you mean? Isn't helping?" she asked.

"Well, watching him today, it looked like Ben's riding Mercury exactly like he rides Red," said Ty.

"But that's the whole idea," said Amy. "That's why I got him involved in the first place. And anyway, you can't blame Ben for what happened out on the trail. It wasn't Ben's fault. He made a good suggestion, and I went with it."

"I know," said Ty. "But he was still thinking too far ahead. Ben's always working toward the next big show with Red. He pushes him so hard. That's fine, because Red wants to respond. But Mercury's not competing anymore. And he's damaged. He needs a different approach."

Amy reached for the reins of one of the bridles and started twisting it between her fingers, thinking hard. "But we don't know yet what's going to get through to Mercury," she said eventually. "Ben and Red have a really special relationship, and Mercury's just as talented and volatile as Red. Ben still has as good a chance of reaching him as we do."

Ty raked a hand through his hair. "You might be right, Amy," he said, sounding uneasy. "But I'm beginning to think we're wrong to be treating Mercury like a competition horse. He's way past that. I think the main thing we should do is to try to heal the hurt. He's been through a lot."

Amy felt astonished and dismayed. "He can't be way past competing, Ty," she protested. "That's what he's here for! Gabriel and Bruce have brought him to us to get him back on track. If we don't think we can do that, we should tell them so."

She paused, thinking of what Mercury was like to work with. She thought of his energy and power and all the talent that lay just beneath the surface. "Anyway," she continued, "you know I agree with you about his needing to heal, but I think he's a natural competitor. Some horses love to compete and jump. They have fire in their blood. I think Mercury's like that, and healing him will mean finding that part of him again."

Ty shrugged, his eyes still troubled. "Well, I guess we'll have to see how it goes," he said quietly. He took Amy's hand and squeezed it. "We can't do any more than that. But I just have this feeling, deep down, that . . ." He stopped, hesitating.

"What?" pressed Amy.

Ty looked at her honestly. "That Mercury will never compete again," he said.

Chapter Four

That night, Amy lay in bed staring at the ceiling, unable to take in what Ty had said. Had he really meant it? If he did, it was almost like saying he didn't believe that Mercury should be at Heartland at all. And she hated feeling like they didn't agree. A wave of confusion swept over her. Ty seemed to be seeing everything so differently — including his relationship with her. He was perfectly happy for everyone to know what was going on between them, whereas she still felt so — so private about it.

Her thoughts drifted to Mercury again. Maybe Ty was right. Maybe Mercury's experiences had changed him too much. Maybe he'd never be the same again.

As she drifted into sleep, the image of Albatross being ridden by Huten came into Amy's mind, the two in perfect harmony. Albatross cantered on, his white tail floating behind him. Then, suddenly, it wasn't Huten riding him anymore but her mother, laughing, her face alive with happiness.

The image brought Amy back out of sleep. She sat up in bed, her head spinning with questions. What was it that Marion had learned with Huten? What had made such a difference to her? In her half-awake state, Amy believed that Marion would have known a cure for Mercury — and Amy was certain she learned it at Ocanumba. Amy wondered if her mother had taken any notes about her experiences there. Maybe she had left a clue.

Amy slid out of bed and tiptoed to her mother's old room, now used as a guest room. She and Lou had finally finished sorting out all of Marion's belongings. That's when Amy had come across *Hearing the Silence*. If Marion had written anything down about Huten and Ocanumba, Amy knew that it would be in one of the tattered notebooks that she'd found in with the book.

Quietly, she switched on the light and took her mother's journals from their drawer. The entries were dated, and Amy found the right year easily. She leafed through the pages eagerly, but she was soon disappointed. Marion had written very little at that time. All Amy found was the date, with "Trip to Ocanumba" written next to it. The following pages were blank.

Amy stared at the book, feeling sad and frustrated.

Not for the first time since her mother had died, she longed to see her one more time and to ask her for advice. But Marion was gone. Amy put the books back in the drawer and crept back to bed, her heart heavy. She lay thinking about Mercury and the differences between herself and Ty. She wondered what Huten would think. Something inside told her he might not agree with either of them exactly. He would have a different way of looking at the problem. *I can't ask Mom, but I wish I could ask Huten*, Amy thought sleepily. *I'm sure he'd have an answer.*

✑

"He really likes that!" commented Ben as Amy worked in T-touch circles up Mercury's neck.

"Yeah, he's lapping it up," agreed Amy, smiling. "He doesn't have any problems relaxing in his stall, for sure. He's almost asleep."

As if to agree, Mercury flicked an ear back lazily and shifted the weight off one of his hind legs.

It was Thursday evening, and Amy was doing her final session of the day with Mercury before going in for supper. Ben leaned on the half door of the stall, frowning.

"I just don't get it," Ben said, looking at Mercury. "Plenty of show horses get rapped. It's not against the rules as long as they only use a bamboo cane. And it's not all that painful for the horse. The idea is that the trainer just taps the horse's forelegs to make him think he's clipped the fence. It only stings a little bit. And the horse learns to jump tighter and higher. I don't understand why he's so wound up."

Amy looked up and saw the frustration on Ben's face.

"I guess they must have used more than a cane on Mercury," she said. "And it's not like it's just a physical thing, anyway. Somehow, they've broken his will to jump."

"I don't think a horse like Mercury ever loses the will to jump," said Ben passionately. "He's born for it. You can just see it in him. He's a real competitor."

Amy sighed and concentrated on the T-touch circles. Somehow, what Ty had said to her earlier kept repeating in her mind. *Mercury will never compete again*. But in her heart, Amy agreed with Ben. They certainly wouldn't find a solution to Mercury's problem by giving up. They had to find another way forward.

"Look," she said to Ben. "Let's do a session with him together tomorrow, when I get home from school, and see how he does. We'll try some different techniques."

Ben looked relieved. "Sounds good to me," he said. "See you later."

He straightened up and left Amy to finish the session. Amy felt anxious. She could sense that Ben really wanted to get somewhere with Mercury. It was only natural — Mercury was the first horse he'd really worked with since coming to Heartland. If they didn't succeed in curing him, he'd take it personally. That's what Ben was like. He needed to win to feel good about himself, and Amy knew he wanted to win with Mercury, too.

"It's not working, Ben," Amy called from where she was perched on the training ring fence. "Take him up to the top end of the ring again."

Mercury had just refused a small jump made of several bales of straw. The sleek gray horse was backing away from the makeshift fence, his head in the air and his eyes rolling. Ben nodded and guided Mercury back to the top area of the ring, which was clear of any jumps or obstacles.

The idea had been to break Mercury's association between poles and jumping. Ben suggested that they introduce Mercury to some nontraditional fences, like the straw, so that the horse wouldn't think of the poles that had rapped his legs. If they could break that connection in Mercury's mind, he might learn to love jumping again.

Amy had agreed that it was worth a try, but it hadn't worked. "I think we should finish up," she called. "Give him ten more minutes on the lunge so that he finishes on a good note."

"OK," said Ben in a resigned voice. "I'll come find you when I'm done."

Amy climbed down from the fence and started walking slowly up to the yard. She hated the expression of disappointment and frustration on Ben's face, but there was nothing she could do about it. She didn't have any answers. Nothing she had tried with Mercury had worked, either. Ben's idea had been a good one; it made perfect sense. It wasn't his fault that it hadn't worked, but it was clear that he didn't see it that way.

"Amy," Ty's voice broke through her thoughts — "can you give me a hand moving some sacks of grain?"

Amy nodded. "Sure," she said, following him to the feed room.

"So Ben's working Mercury?" asked Ty, grasping a sack firmly.

"Yeah," Amy replied. "But there's still no progress. Mercury's not responding, and Ben's blaming himself. He thinks it's his fault."

"Well, maybe it is," said Ty evenly. "I still think he's taking the wrong approach."

"Ty!" protested Amy. "He discusses everything he does with me first. He suggests all the things that we would try. Ben has great ideas."

"I don't mean it like that," said Ty. "I just think that it's useless to keep pointing Mercury at fences when he doesn't want to jump."

"But that's why he's here," insisted Amy. "If we avoid the jumping issue, we're avoiding the problem, and we won't be able to cure Mercury."

"Well, maybe he doesn't need to be cured," said Ty irritably.

"What do you mean by that?" Amy snapped back. She and Ty had never disagreed about a horse's treatment. Amy had never been so confused, and yet she was sure she was right. She hoisted a sack across the feed room and pushed it angrily against the others. She and Ty worked in silence for a few minutes, the atmosphere charged.

Then Amy sighed. "Sorry," she said, not knowing what else to say.

Ty straightened up from the sacks and nodded. "I know," he said. "I'm sorry, too."

Amy took a deep breath. "You know, I've been thinking," she paused. "About Huten."

"Huten?" asked Ty.

"At Ocanumba," said Amy. "I'd like to ask him for help."

"Not a bad idea," said Ty. "Why don't you give him a call?"

"Well . . ." Amy hesitated. "I'm not sure how much use that would be. I was thinking I'd like to take Mercury up there. To Ten Beeches."

Ty stared at her. "What?" he asked in astonishment.

"I know it's a long shot," Amy said hurriedly. "But I've seen how Huten works. He has a special way of putting horses back in touch with themselves when they've been damaged. If anyone can judge whether Mercury will ever jump again, it's Huten."

Ty was still looking at her in disbelief. "Amy," he said, "transporting a horse is a big liability. Not to mention how that kind of ride might affect a damaged horse. We're responsible for Mercury's well-being. How do you think the owners are going to react if we tell them we can't do anything for Mercury and our last hope is taking him to an old mystic in the mountains?"

"Huten isn't a mystic," Amy objected.

"I know he isn't," said Ty. "But Gabriel and Bruce may not understand that. All they'll know is that we failed here at Heartland. I think they'll feel like we're resorting to desperate measures."

Amy frowned. There was something in what Ty was saying. Taking a horse somewhere else wouldn't be the best thing for Heartland's reputation.

"And anyway," added Ty, "what about Ben? Aren't you worried about his feelings? How will he react if you take Mercury away?"

Amy swallowed. Everything Ty was saying made sense. But now that she'd put her idea into words, going to Ocanumba seemed like a real possibility. She shrugged. "I just think we have to consider every option," she said.

"For the horse's sake. After all, that's what we're here for."

🙰

"Soraya, tell me if I'm being crazy," Amy said to her friend the next day as they sat outside during the school lunch hour. "I've got this idea into my head about Mercury, and it won't go away."

"Don't tell me," said Soraya. "You're still thinking about Ocanumba."

"How did you guess?" asked Amy in amazement.

"I'm not sure," said Soraya. "I think it was the way you talked about it when you got back. That place sure made an impression on you."

"Yeah," agreed Amy. "But not everyone thinks it's a good idea."

"You mean Ty," said Soraya perceptively.

"Mmm. Right again. He's not too sure about it," admitted Amy. "In fact . . ." She felt her cheeks grow hot and trailed off.

"What?" probed Soraya gently.

"Things aren't that great between us right now," said Amy. "We don't agree on how to treat Mercury. And I don't know how to deal with everyone knowing about us."

"Why?" asked Soraya. "You two are perfect together."

"I — I know," said Amy awkwardly. "But it's really different, having everything out in the open. There are people like Ashley to deal with, for a start. But it's more than that. I just kind of get embarrassed. Like people think we're going to be holding hands the whole time or something dumb like that."

Soraya's face creased into laughter at the idea. "You and Ty aren't at all like that," she said. "No one's thinking you're going to change just because you have a boyfriend, Amy. And anyway, even if they are, why should you care?"

"That's what Ty says," said Amy. "But, I don't know, I guess with everyone knowing, it makes it feel too real — too established. It kind of makes me nervous."

Soraya's face became serious again. She thought for a minute, then said, "Well, you know, if that's how you feel, maybe a trip to Ocanumba is just what you need. It'd give you some space to think things through."

"Do you think so?" asked Amy. Soraya's words filled her with relief.

"Why not? It makes sense to me." said Soraya. "But have you asked Lou? Or your grandpa?"

"No," said Amy. "Not yet."

"Well, you can't go unless they agree," said Soraya. "So I guess that'll be the deciding factor."

That evening, Amy decided to go for a ride on her own, up on the trails. She wanted time to think. She took

Sundance, as she rarely had time to ride him now that Heartland was so busy.

She saddled him up and set off down the track that led past the training rings. In the smaller ring, she could see Ben riding Red, taking him over a small course of jumps. She brought Sundance to a halt and watched for a minute. Ben and Red were a great pair and were always a pleasure to watch.

Ben had set up a difficult course of jumps, but they were nothing that Red couldn't handle. He sailed over much more difficult courses to win at local shows. But something was going wrong. As Amy watched, Ben turned a tight corner after an Oxer and rode Red at a difficult double. From where she was sitting, Amy could see that the angle was too tight. Red wasn't going to be able to find his stride quickly enough. He was unbalanced and skidded to a halt in front of the fence. Annoyed, Ben pulled him around in a tight circle and rode at the double again.

Amy could see that Red was tensing up. He was feeling wary of the double because he hadn't been able to jump it the first time. Now he was being pushed at it again. He made an awkward leap into the air and landed off balance. He wasn't ready for the second fence in the combination and refused again.

Amy was surprised. She hadn't seen Ben ride so badly for a long while, if ever. And she was even more surprised when he pulled the chestnut up sharply and yanked him in the mouth, backing him up. Red was fighting, uncertain what was wanted from him, but Ben turned him around so that he could approach the double again.

"Ben!" Amy called. She couldn't help herself, even though she knew she shouldn't interfere.

Ben looked around to see who had called him, his face taut with tension and determination. He saw Amy but didn't ride over to her.

"He's confused!" Amy called as Ben turned Red toward the fences. Ben, with his upper body hunched forward, pounded Red with his heels. Red surged ahead. He took the first fence too early, but again made it over. Ben closed his legs around the sweating horse's sides and pushed him on to the second. Red scrambled over but knocked the top pole, and it clattered to the ground.

Ben let his shoulders relax slightly, and as he rode past again, Amy saw a shameful expression on his face. He knew as well as Amy that he was doing all the things that would make a sensitive horse tense up. He cantered Red around the ring, letting him relax. Then he turned him toward an easy fence. Red hopped over it, back to his usual eager manner. Amy sighed with relief as Red now slowed to a trot. Ben stroked his horse's lathered neck but didn't look in Amy's direction.

Hastily, Amy rode Sundance up the track and onto the trails. She could see that Ben was embarrassed and didn't want to talk to her. She nudged Sundance into a trot, thinking furiously. Why was Ben so impatient with Red all of a sudden? Was Ben's riding affected by his work with Mercury? It would make sense. Ben was the sort of person who needs everything to be going well. But whatever the reasons, Amy realized she had made up her own mind. She had to put the issues with Ben aside. She was going to ask Lou and Grandpa about going to Ocanumba as soon as possible.

"More scrambled eggs, anyone?" asked Grandpa, gesturing with a wooden spoon. "There's just a spoonful left — still hot."

"Over here, Jack, please," said Ty. It was Sunday morning, and everyone was gathered in the kitchen for breakfast. Grandpa always prepared a feast — baked ham and scrambled eggs and pancakes, orange juice and coffee.

This Sunday, though, the atmosphere was quieter than usual. Lou and Grandpa were being chatty and cheerful, but Ben wasn't saying much, and Amy still felt awkward when she and Ty were around other people. But that wasn't all. She had decided that this was prob-ably the best time to raise the question of Mercury —

while they were all together. She felt nervous and just picked at her blueberry muffin.

"Amy?" asked Lou, between sips of coffee. "You're usually starving. What's wrong?"

"Nothing," Amy said hurriedly. She gathered her thoughts and took the plunge. "I've just been thinking a lot about Mercury."

Ben and Ty looked at her quickly. Amy noticed a frown on Ty's face.

Grandpa looked at her inquiringly.

"Isn't it going well?" he asked.

"We just don't seem to be getting through to him," said Amy. "Nothing seems to work. Ben's had some really good ideas but no results. So I was wondering about Huten, at Ocanumba."

"What about him?" asked Lou, puzzled.

"Whether he'd be able to help," said Amy.

"But how can he help?" persisted Lou. She looked at Amy suspiciously. "This doesn't have anything to do with that promise stuff he talked about, does it?"

Amy took a deep breath. "No," she said. "Not really. But I am wondering whether I could take Mercury to his stable."

"What!" exclaimed Lou. She put down her knife and fork. "It's miles away! We can't just go sending horses off around the country if we can't cure them ourselves."

"I know, I know," said Amy. She looked anxiously

around the table. Ben looked shocked and miserable, while Grandpa had raised his eyebrows in contemplation. "I talked to Ty about it, and he doesn't think it's a good idea, either," she said honestly, throwing a glance in Ty's direction. "But I just wanted to see what everyone else thought. I know it seems like a crazy idea, but I think Mom might have gone for it. I have this feeling that Huten might understand how the rapping affected Mercury psychologically. I think it could be Mercury's only chance."

Lou sighed. "Amy, I told you what I thought about that promise that Mom made. There were probably a thousand very good reasons why she never went back. We don't even know what she said, exactly. It's not fair of him to make you feel guilty over it. Besides, it's not up to you to fulfill promises Mom didn't keep."

"This has nothing to do with Mom," said Amy. "At least nothing to do with her promise, anyway. It has to do with Mercury. I think that the way Huten works is really special and that Mom learned something important from it. I can't ask Mom what that was. But I think that if anyone can reach Mercury, Huten can."

Silence fell around the table for a few minutes.

"Have you considered what his owners might say?" asked Grandpa eventually.

"Well," said Amy, "we'd have to explain the situation

to them. They might say no. But I wanted to talk to everyone here first."

She looked quickly at Ben again. His expression was blank, and he mechanically carried on eating his breakfast. Amy felt bad and wished she'd spoken to him first. It must seem like she was just taking over and not giving him a say.

As if he was reading her thoughts, Ty asked Ben in a quiet voice, "What do you think, Ben?"

Ben looked up and shrugged. "I don't know," he said a bit stiffly. "I agree he hasn't been making much progress. But I guess it's not for me to say."

Amy heard the disillusionment in his words and felt even worse.

"It's not anyone's fault that we're not getting through to Mercury," she said.

"I don't see how you can be sure that Huten will get through to him, either," said Lou. "It's a big risk to take, isn't it? And it's also an expensive one."

"Lou, you didn't see him working with Albatross," said Amy. "It was really amazing." She looked again at Grandpa, who was frowning thoughtfully. "Grandpa, how do you feel about it?"

To Amy's surprise, he didn't dismiss the idea entirely. "It would be an unusual step for us to take," he said. "But that doesn't mean we shouldn't take it. I'd like to give it some thought. And in the meantime, keep on trying to make progress with Mercury," he said.

"OK, Grandpa," said Amy, feeling relieved. But then she stole a glance at Ty. His lips were pursed, and she could tell that he still thought it was a bad idea. Her heart sank a little. She hated being on bad terms with him — and it was so unusual for them to disagree so much. What was going wrong?

❧

After breakfast, Ben left the table quickly and went out onto the yard, followed by Ty. Amy stayed in the kitchen to help Lou with the dishes.

"Sorry if I seemed really negative," Lou said awkwardly after a few minutes. "It just seems like a drastic thing to do."

"I understand," said Amy. "It doesn't make much sense from the outside. But I keep thinking about the way that Huten works, and I feel sure he can help Mercury."

"But you don't know that," said Lou. "What if he can't? Then what?"

Amy looked at her sister honestly. "I don't know, Lou," she said in a low voice. "Anyway, I don't know if I'm even going yet."

She finished putting the dishes away and headed out onto the yard. Maddison was in need of some exercise, so she made her way to the back barn with his lunging bridle.

In the barn, Ty was mucking out Jigsaw's stall.

"Hi," Amy said awkwardly. "How's it going?"

Ty looked up at her briefly. "Well, apart from the fact that Ben appears to have forgotten how to ride and you're planning a wild-goose chase, everything's fine," he said sardonically.

Amy tried to ignore his tone. "You've been watching Ben and Red?" she asked. "I noticed they're out of sync."

Ty snorted. "You could say that." He lifted a forkful of bedding and shook it angrily.

Amy watched him, wondering what to say. She could tell that he was angry with her, but she didn't know what to do about it. "Ty," she began hesitantly, after a pause, "I know you don't want me to take Mercury away."

Ty glared at her. "I keep thinking that I have a say in what goes on around here, Amy," he said. "But then I find out that I don't. Sure, you'll ask me questions and talk about things, but in the end, you do whatever you want to do."

Amy was horrified. "That's not true!" she exclaimed. She grasped for the first thing that came into her head. "How can you say that? You know it's not true. You're just jealous because I've been working so much with Ben and Mercury. And now you don't want me to go away."

She saw a wounded look flash across Ty's face and instantly regretted what she'd said. She hadn't even meant it. But it was too late. Ty picked up the wheelbarrow.

"You're welcome to think that, Amy," he muttered as he walked past her. "Think exactly what you like. It's not like I can stop you from doing what you want."

Chapter Five

There was a soft knock on Amy's bedroom door. "Amy? Are you in there?" Grandpa's gruff voice called.

Amy threw her magazine to one side and got up from her bed. It was after supper on Sunday evening, and Amy had disappeared up to her room. Her argument with Ty had made her feel miserable, and she hadn't really felt like being with anyone.

"Are you OK, honey?" asked Grandpa as she opened the door.

Amy smiled wanly. "I'm fine, Grandpa," she said. "Do you need me for something?"

"I'm going to make some hot chocolate," said Grandpa. "Do you want some?"

"That sounds good," agreed Amy.

She followed Grandpa into the kitchen and sat down at the table while he brought the milk from the fridge.

"I wanted to talk to you about Mercury. I've spent all day mulling it over," said Grandpa, pouring the milk into a pan. "And I think you should go."

Amy's mouth dropped open. Deep down, she hadn't really expected anyone to agree to the trip. It had all seemed a bit unreal — like something that lay just out of reach.

"We'll need to talk to your school. They may not allow a trip like this," Grandpa carried on. "You can't fall behind with your schoolwork. But I'll call them in the morning. We'll also have to think about Mercury's owners. We need to explain the situation to them, the sooner the better. If they agree, I think you should go for a week or so and see how it works out."

"Grandpa, you're wonderful!" said Amy. She got up and hugged him. "Thank you. I'll call Gabriel and Bruce tomorrow, right after school. And Huten, too."

"I trust your instincts, Amy," Grandpa said, returning her hug. "And I know what a big effect going to Ten Beeches had on your mom. If you feel Huten holds the key to helping Mercury, I hope you're right."

Amy smiled, feeling that a huge weight had been lifted off her mind. "I didn't expect anyone to agree with me,

Grandpa," she said. She hesitated. "I seem to be getting everything wrong just now."

Grandpa looked at her fondly. "We all have times like that, Amy," he said. "It'll work out in the long run. Think of all the difficult times we've come through in the last few months."

"I guess," Amy said thoughtfully, watching Grandpa pour the chocolate into mugs.

"Hey, I smell something good," said Lou, walking into the kitchen.

Grandpa smiled. "There's some left over. Would you like a cup?"

"Mmm. Please," said Lou.

"Grandpa thinks I should go to Huten's stable," said Amy.

Lou looked startled. "Oh — really?" she added, looking questioningly at Grandpa. "Well, I guess there's nothing I can say," she said, with an edge of irritation in her voice.

Grandpa passed Amy the mugs of chocolate, then sat down.

"We'll need to talk it over with a few people first," he said. "It'll take some arranging. But I don't see why it shouldn't work."

"Well, I hope you have a good trip," Lou said grudgingly to Amy. "But I can't see why you're so set on it."

❧

"So what did she say?" Soraya asked curiously as Amy came out of the principal's office Monday morning.

Amy grinned happily. "She's agreed to it," she said. "Grandpa called her earlier and persuaded her. But only if I take all my schoolwork with me. And I can't be gone for more than a week."

"Will that be enough?" asked Soraya.

"It'll have to be," said Amy. "I don't think Heartland can spare me for any longer than that, anyway." Her face creased into a frown as she thought about it all. Her trip was going to create a lot of work for everyone else. Ty and Ben would have to cover all her work between them.

"Everyone's agreed it's a good idea, though, haven't they?" asked Soraya. "I mean, Ty and Ben."

"Well — mostly," she said uncomfortably. "But then they don't know I'm going yet, not definitely."

"If it's any use, I can go to Heartland after school every afternoon and help out," offered Soraya.

Amy squeezed her friend's arm. "Would you?" she said gratefully. "That would be absolutely wonderful. I couldn't thank you enough. Are you sure?"

"Of course I'm sure," said Soraya. She grinned, slightly sheepishly.

Amy laughed. "Well, I know one person on the yard will be very happy about that," she said. "Maybe then he'll forgive me for going."

"You mean Ben? Do you really think he'll be happy?" asked Soraya, blushing slightly.

"Come on, Soraya, you know he will," said Amy. "Ben's like a different person when you're around. It's good to see him laugh with you. He takes life so seriously."

Soraya smiled gratefully at Amy, and Amy thought ahead to the afternoon. She hoped Ben would take the news about Ten Beeches well.

❧

Amy waited impatiently for someone to answer the phone. Eventually, she heard a familiar voice on the other end.

"Barbara?" she asked.

"Yes, speaking," said the voice.

"Barbara, it's Amy Fleming, from Heartland. I visited Ten Beeches with my sister last weekend. I was wondering if I could speak to Huten."

"Oh, hello, Amy. I'll call him in," said Barbara. "I know he'll be pleased to hear from you."

Amy took a deep breath. Now that she'd gone so far with this, it would be a real disappointment if Huten didn't want her to come. She'd already spoken to Gabriel, who had agreed to the trip. Amy heard footsteps at the other end of the line.

"Huten, it's Amy, Marion's daughter," she said as she heard him pick up the receiver.

"Amy," said Huten. "How can I help?"

"I — I was wondering if I could come and work with you. With one of our horses."

"Well, there's plenty of room," said Huten. He didn't sound at all surprised. "Tell me about the horse."

Amy's heart leaped. Quickly, she explained Mercury's problem and what they'd tried so far. Huten made no comment but simply asked, "When do you think you might come?"

"We need to move on things as quickly as possible," Amy said. "I was thinking of maybe this Saturday. For a week."

"I'll look forward to working with you, Amy," said Huten in his measured tone. "Travel safely."

As Amy put down the phone, she felt a surge of excitement flood through her. She went into the den, where Lou and Grandpa were watching TV.

"It's all set," she exclaimed. "I can go!"

"That's good news. I can drive you there," said Grandpa, smiling at Amy's excitement. "That's probably the best plan, so we don't disrupt the stable work."

"Thanks again, Grandpa," said Amy.

She hurried out onto the yard to find Ty before he left for the night. She felt such an odd mix of things. Despite her excitement about going to Ten Beeches, her heart sank at the thought of what Ty would say about the news. They hadn't talked since their argument. Amy hardly knew how to break it to him.

Ty was just climbing into his pickup. Amy went up to the window as he pulled on his seat belt.

"Ty," she called, tapping on the glass.

Ty wound down the window.

Amy looked at him awkwardly.

"You're going home?" she asked, stating the obvious.

Ty nodded.

"I just wanted to let you know, it looks like I'm going to Ocanumba on Saturday. For a week," she told him. "Gabriel thought it was a good idea, and Grandpa's going to drive me." The words sounded strange and flat. All the excitement drained out of them.

Ty smiled coolly. "Right," he said. "Well, I guess that's settled."

"Yeah," said Amy. His distant expression made her heart feel stiff. She paused. "Soraya's offered to help around the yard while I'm gone."

"That's nice of her," said Ty. "That'll help." He started the engine, and Amy stepped back. "See you tomorrow," he said.

"Yeah," said Amy, hesitating. She wanted to add

something else — something to make everything right again. But she couldn't find the words. She didn't know what they'd be. "See you," she added.

Ty nodded, and the pickup began to move forward. With her head lowered, Amy turned back toward the farmhouse.

By Thursday, Amy was beginning to feel exhausted. On top of all the usual chores, she was swamped with homework. She barely had time to do her usual studying, and now she was having to do more. She had to take two tests before she left. Every night, she worked until midnight, then got up at six to start mucking out the stalls, mixing the feeds, grooming, and all the other chores that needed to be done before she went to school.

Most important of all, though, she was spending as much time with Mercury as possible so that she would have a good relationship with him before they left. After school that night, she came home and took him from his stall. As she led him up the yard, Ben came out of Red's stall, and she waved to him. He waved back.

"Hey, Ben," she called. "I'm about to work with Mercury. Do you want to come and help me?"

Ben paused. The expression on his face was difficult to read. With a shake of his head, he sighed.

"Amy — I think it's probably better if I don't," he said.

Amy looked anxious. "I'm not going to try any jumping work," she said. "I was going to do some work on the lunge, then maybe join up. I want Mercury to trust me as much as possible before we go."

Ben hesitated, then shook his head. "Thanks, Amy," he said. "I know it hasn't been easy deciding what to do with Mercury. And I don't think I was much help." He sighed. "I've got to try to figure what's wrong with Red now, so I'd like to concentrate on that for a while — if it's OK with you."

Amy nodded, feeling bad. "Of course it is," she said. "Well — see you later."

She led Mercury down to the training ring, trying to ignore the waves of fatigue rolling over her. As she started work, Mercury seemed restless, tossing his head as he trotted around the ring. It was natural, Amy knew — he was picking up on the fact that she was tired. But as she concentrated on the horse, she felt her energy reviving, and he settled into a pleasant rhythm.

"That's a boy," she murmured, urging him into a canter.

Out of the corner of her eye, she became aware of a figure watching her at the edge of the training ring. She brought Mercury back to a trot and turned to see Lou standing there.

"Hi, Lou," called Amy. "Did you need something?"

"No, no," said Lou, appearing a bit embarrassed. "I was just watching. Mercury looks like he's going well."

"He's settled down now," agreed Amy, pleased that Lou was taking an interest. It helped, even if she still didn't agree about the trip to Ten Beeches. She brought Mercury to a halt. "I'm going to do some lunging with him," she added. "Would you like to try?"

"Me?" asked Lou, astonished.

"Why not?" asked Amy.

Lou shrugged, and Amy saw a strange expression cross her face — a mixture of apprehension and excitement. But it quickly disappeared. "Well —" she began.

"Come on," said Amy. "You won't believe how quickly it'll come back to you."

Lou climbed over the fence and approached the center of the ring nervously.

"Make a V with the longline and the lunging whip," Amy said as she handed them to Lou. "That's it."

Lou clicked her tongue to tell Mercury to move into a walk. He obeyed willingly, and Lou soon had him circling around in a smooth trot. Amy sneaked a look at her sister's expression. She was looking proud and flushed. Things had really begun to change since their father, Tim, had visited a few weeks before and Lou had tried join up. For the first time since she was a child, she was really working with horses again. And now, as Lou concentrated on the circling horse, a thought occurred to Amy. Maybe she was ready to take the biggest step of all — getting onto a horse's back again.

As Lou brought Mercury to a halt, Amy decided to suggest it.

"Lou," she said, "why don't you get up on his back? I'd hold on to him. He's really calm."

Lou sized up the horse and took a deep breath. Then she shook her head. "Thanks, Amy," she said shortly. "The lunging was great, but I'm not ready to ride again."

"You could just walk," persisted Amy gently. "I really wouldn't let him go. It'll be fine."

Lou hesitated. "Well," she said reluctantly, "all right, but just as long as you hold on to him."

"I will," Amy promised.

She gave Lou a leg up, and Lou effortlessly settled herself on Mercury's bare back. As she took up the slack in the reins, Amy looked at her in amazement. She could tell, already, that Lou had a perfect seat. But why did she feel so surprised? Lou had ridden almost every day until the age of twelve. It was instinctual — even if it had been a long time.

They walked sedately around the training ring, with Amy holding firmly on to the bridle. "So what do you think?" asked Amy. "Want to try a trot?"

Despite herself, Lou's face broke into a smile. "OK," she said. "But I'd better not fall off, or it's all your fault!"

"You won't," Amy assured her, stifling a laugh. "He has a really smooth stride."

Amy broke into a jog alongside the gelding as he increased his pace. They did a half circuit of the ring, with Lou settling comfortably into the rhythm. Then Amy brought Mercury to a walk and back to a halt.

Lou slithered off his back. For an instant, her eyes filled with tears, but she blinked them back. "Amy, that was great," she said, hugging her sister. "Thanks." She smiled. "I can hardly believe it. I never thought I'd ride again. Even after I did the join up and Daddy left, I still didn't think I could do it."

Amy smiled back, happiness welling up inside her.

Quickly, Lou regained her composure. She patted Mercury's neck thoughtfully and turned back to Amy, her expression serious. "You remember what Huten said when we visited," she said in a low voice. "About how it can be hard to find the right time?"

Amy nodded.

"Well," said Lou, struggling to find the words, "I — I think you spotted the right time just now. For me. I don't think I would have known it myself."

Amy looked at her sister thoughtfully.

"And I hope Ten Beeches works out," Lou carried on, in a rush. "I'll be thinking of you."

"Thanks," said Amy, smiling warmly at her sister. "I'll be thinking of you, too."

🐝

It was Friday night. Amy and Grandpa were leaving first thing in the morning, and she was just packing her suitcase now.

"Have you said good-bye to Ty?" asked Lou, standing at Amy's bedroom door with a sandwich. Amy hadn't even had time to sit down for a proper supper. "He'll be leaving soon."

Amy looked up desperately. "What time is it?" she asked.

"Almost nine-thirty," said Lou.

"Oh, no," groaned Amy. "I'd better go find him."

She left her half-packed suitcase on the bed and the sandwich on her dresser and went down to the yard. "Ty!" she called. He wasn't out front, so she went to the back barn. She found him coming out of Pirate's stall with some hoof medication.

"I just came to say good-bye," said Amy awkwardly. "I probably won't see you in the morning. Well, not for very long."

Ty put the grooming kit down. "Oh — right." He paused, and there was a silence. Amy met his gaze for a minute.

"I hope you find the answers you're looking for," said Ty.

"Thanks. I hope things go OK here without me," Amy said awkwardly.

"We'll miss you," said Ty, "but we'll be fine."

There was another silence, both of them searching for something else to say.

"Well — I'd better get back to my packing," said Amy. "I'm still only half finished, and I'm sure I'm forgetting things already."

"See you," said Ty.

"Bye," said Amy. She turned, and hurried back toward the house, tears blinding her eyes before she was out of the stable block.

❧

Amy slept badly, tossing and turning. She got up as soon as it was light, anxious to get on the road. When she and Grandpa were finally on their way, exhaustion overcame her and she slept. Jack Bartlett drove the trailer steadily, and when she woke they were only about half an hour from Huten's stable.

"Grandpa! Why didn't you wake me up?" asked Amy. "You've been driving for hours without any company."

"That's OK," said Grandpa. "You looked like you needed the rest, and I had the radio. A little solitude never hurt anyone."

Amy looked out the window. They were already well into the mountains. As they rounded a bend, a deep forest appeared before them, and the reality of what she was doing began to sink in. It would be her first time on her own away from Heartland since Marion died, and a ripple of apprehension ran through her. This was going to be so different from her weekend break with Lou.

"It's going to be a challenging week," she commented.

"Yes," said Grandpa. "But we're only a phone call away if you need to talk to us. You know, I'm really proud of you, Amy."

"Thanks, Grandpa," Amy said gratefully. She thought of Ty, and sadness filled her. If only he'd said something similar before she'd left. But he hadn't. Amy had to face the fact that, for once, they weren't getting along. A cold feeling clutched at her heart. It was exactly what she'd feared would happen — that if they started dating, things would go wrong. Would it ever be the same between them again?

❧

As they turned into the road approaching Ten Beeches, Amy tried to focus on the week ahead. Huten and Bill Whitepath stood waiting as the trailer pulled up. Huten raised his hand and smiled. Amy jumped out of the truck and made the introductions.

"Good to see you, Amy," said Huten.

Jack Bartlett shook their hands in turn, and Bill helped them unload Mercury.

"He'll be going in the end stall. We'll settle him in, then I'll show you where you're going to stay."

Mercury looked interested in his new surroundings. A couple of the other horses neighed and snorted in the direction of the new arrival, and he squealed in return. His stall was large and airy, with plenty of fresh straw on the floor, and he was soon happily munching on his hay net.

Barbara appeared at the door of the cabin as they walked up the path, a big smile of welcome on her face.

"Come on in," she said. "Hope you had a nice drive."

She ushered them through to the kitchen. "First things first," she said, placing steaming bowls of soup in front of them. "Lunch is ready."

Grandpa winked at Amy reassuringly as they sat down. She grinned, but inside she was beginning to fill with apprehension.

When he'd finished his soup, Grandpa stood. "Well, I've got a long drive back," he said, "I'd better be going. Thanks for the food."

Barbara nodded as Amy went out with him to the trailer. He hugged her, then climbed into the driver's seat. "Take care of yourself," he said as he put the truck into gear.

"I will," said Amy.

"Let us know how it's going," he added.

Amy nodded speechlessly, waving as the trailer moved forward. A lump rose in her throat. This was it. She was on her own. She swallowed, then turned back to the cabin.

❧

"I'll show you your room. It's where you and your mother stayed when you were young," said Barbara, "at the far end of the cabin." She led Amy to a small but cozy room that had a view into the trees. It was simply furnished, with a bed, a chest of drawers, and a wardrobe. The chest and the wardrobe were painted eggshell blue.

Amy put her suitcase on the bed. "Thank you," she said. "It's lovely."

"Glad you like it. I'll let you get your bearings," said Barbara. "Give me a shout if you need anything."

Amy went to the window. She opened it and stared out into the forest. It was so quiet. Beyond the beeches surrounding the cabin, a rich variety of trees grew densely together, making the forest look impenetrable. As she peered through the trees, a wave of doubt came over her. What was she doing here? She had brought a horse to a place she didn't know, to people she'd met only twice — the first time when she was just six. And she would be here on her own, without any of the people she loved and who had supported her so strongly over the last months.

Why had she been so certain that this was such a good idea?

Chapter Six

Amy unpacked her suitcase slowly, then sat on her bed and looked out the window. The first thing she should do, she decided, was find Huten and talk to him about Mercury. Then at least she'd get some idea of how things worked around here.

She put on her work jeans and headed out onto the yard. Huten was picking out the feet of a roan mare and straightened up as she approached. He moved around to the other side of the mare and picked up her other hind leg. Amy watched him as he worked, seeing how gnarled his hands were. But his motions were smooth and steady. She guessed he must be nearly eighty, with a lifetime of experience with horses.

He finished the mare's feet without speaking, giving

her a light pat on her withers. Then he led her back into her stall. Amy trailed after him, feeling uncertain.

"I was wondering if you'd like to take a look at Mercury," she said. "Maybe I could tell you how we've been working with him."

Huten regarded her calmly. "There's plenty of time for that," he said. "It's more important that you settle in. Relax. Take a look around."

But I've only got a week, thought Amy. She opened her mouth to say just that, but the steady look on Huten's face stopped her. The words died on her lips. Huten gave her a gentle smile and walked slowly off toward the cabin, his back only slightly stooped with age.

Amy watched him go, then wandered around the back of the stables. *Relax,* he'd said. She certainly didn't feel very relaxed — she could feel a knot of anxiety gnawing at her insides. Until she got to work on what she'd come to do, how could she be sure that she'd made the right decision?

She followed a little track into the forest. It soon started to run alongside a little stream, and she sat down on a rock, lost in her thoughts. Ty's face seemed to dance before her as she stared at a boulder in the water. The thought of Ty made Amy's head spin with confusion. There was an uneasiness at the back of her mind. *It's my fault,* a voice whispered. *I've been pushing him away. I'm too stubborn.* Then another voice whispered, *You can't spend all week thinking about Ty. You have to do what you've come here to do.*

She stood up and headed back to the stable yard. Wandering past the stalls, she stopped at Maverick's. She peered inside, expecting to see the wiry, nervous pony that had captured her heart on her previous visit. But he wasn't there. His stall was empty.

Disappointed, she sat on an upturned bucket outside Mercury's stall and wondered what to do. Grandpa might have made it back to Heartland by now. She pulled her cell phone out of her pocket and quickly punched in the familiar number. Lou answered.

"Hi, Lou!" said Amy. "It's me. Is Grandpa home yet?"

"He got back about half an hour ago," said Lou. "He seems pretty tired. How are you?"

"I'm fine," said Amy. But she knew her voice sounded small and lost. Lou seemed so far away. "Nothing much has happened yet."

"Well, give it a chance," said Lou gently. "You just got there."

"Yeah," said Amy. "Well, I just wanted to check on Grandpa. I'd better go."

"Take care," said Lou.

"Thanks, Lou," Amy said gratefully.

She finished the call and sat staring at her phone for a minute. She wondered whether to call Ty as well, but then she decided against it. She wasn't sure what to say; she needed some time to think. She quickly snapped the phone shut and put it back into her pocket. As she did so, she became aware of a shadow nearby. She looked up. Carey was watching her, shielding her eyes from the sun.

Amy smiled at her. "Hi," she said. "Remember me?"

Carey shrugged. "Yeah," she said, in an offhand tone. "You're the one who works with horses."

"Yeah, that's me," Amy agreed, unsure what to make of Carey. She seemed so thorny. Amy got to her feet. Carey didn't seem to be doing anything in particular, and the two girls wandered through the yard, then down the path toward the big training ring where Amy had first watched Huten on Albatross. Carey was silent, and Amy hunted for something to say.

"Do you work with the horses, too?" she asked.

Carey shook her head. "Not much," she said. "I ride sometimes. But it's not really my thing. I'll be leaving this time next year."

Amy felt the same curiosity that she'd felt before. She couldn't imagine having someone like Huten as a grandfather and not completely loving the work he did. "Where are you going to go?" she asked.

"Probably Boston," said Carey. "Or maybe New York. I want to live in the city. I guess I'll go where I find a job." She kicked at a pebble and laughed. "Freedom!" she exclaimed. "I can't wait."

Amy was astonished. "It feels pretty free up here," she commented.

Carey snorted. "For some people, maybe," she said. "But not when you've been here all your life. There's nothing to do." She shrugged, then stared at Amy. "I know you've come to see how Granddad works. You want to tap into his wisdom somehow. But if you ask me, we're better off letting go of the past. My family are far too hooked into all that. A lot of people are like that around here."

"But you have so much history," Amy said uncertainly. "It'll be part of you wherever you go."

Carey made a face. "I'd rather think about the future," she said. "OK, so I'm Native American. *American*. Just like you're American, and a whole bunch of other people are American, people who came from all over. I just want to get on with life like there's no difference. That way we'll all be happy — not by clinging to ancient debts and mind-sets. I want to live for today, for the future."

Amy pondered Carey's words for a few minutes. "Well, I guess there's nothing wrong with that," she said slowly. She looked around herself, taking in the towering poplar and maple trees and the mountainside rising up to one side of them. "But I still think you have something pretty unique here."

Carey snapped a twig from an overhanging branch

and played with it, breaking it up and tossing the pieces into the air. "Plenty of tourists think so, too," she said dryly.

They reached a big turnout paddock beyond the training ring and Amy spotted Maverick. He was the only horse in the paddock and was grazing on his own near the gate. As Amy and Carey approached, he flung his head in the air and stopped chewing his mouthful of grass. Amy leaned over the gate, and he started, then cantered off to the far end of the paddock.

"He's one unhappy pony," Amy said sadly. She looked at Carey, who nodded noncommittally.

"He's still pretty wild," said Carey in a distant tone.

They watched him for a moment. He was still staring at them, unable to continue grazing. *I'd love to try gentling him*, Amy thought to herself. But it was hardly her place to get involved with all the other horses here. She was here for Mercury — and Mercury was the horse she'd have to concentrate on.

"He was really badly neglected," Carey said suddenly. "Some developers found him on this run-down homestead. He'd been part of a herd of these semiwild horses. But the land where they grazed had been pretty well stripped. Maverick was at the bottom of the pecking order, and the other horses bullied him so badly he could barely get enough grass."

Amy looked at Carey in astonishment. For someone who didn't have much to do with the horses, she knew a lot about this one.

"So he's really scared of everything," said Amy. "Including humans."

"Yeah," said Carey. "And other horses here pick up on his fear. We can't let him graze with them yet. He'd just get bullied again."

"So how's he being treated?" asked Amy.

But suddenly, Carey seemed to lose interest again. She was silent for a few moments, then shrugged. "That's Granddad's department," she said, dismissively. She turned away from the gate. "Come on, let's go eat. Ma will have cooked something good."

Over supper, Amy realized that she was exhausted. It had been a long day, and an even longer week had come before it. She ate in silence, her mind too full to join in with the easy family conversation taking place around the table. Barbara smiled warmly at her, and Amy felt that she, at least, understood that weariness had overtaken her. Amy excused herself as quickly as she could and went to her room. There, she was soon sleeping a deep, dreamless sleep.

She was woken by the yellow light filtering through the beech trees outside. She lay for a few minutes, taking in the fact that she was not in her own bed at Heartland. Then she rose, dressed quickly, and headed onto the yard.

"Hello, boy," she said to Mercury, letting herself into his stall. He gave a nicker of welcome, and she rubbed him gently between the eyes and on his neck. His eyes were calm and bright — it seemed that the long journey the day before hadn't bothered him in the slightest. "You've settled in, haven't you?" she murmured to him. He nuzzled her pockets hoping for mints. "More quickly than I have, that's for sure," she added as she fished one out for him. "We'll do some work after breakfast, how'd you like that?"

Mercury turned to his hay net, and Amy let herself back out onto the yard. She spotted Bill carrying some buckets of water and offered to help.

"Sure," he said. "Thanks. You could sweep the yard. And fill some of the hay nets."

Amy felt relieved. At least she was doing something, even if it wasn't what she was here for. She busied herself until it was time for breakfast. *Maybe Huten will talk to me about Mercury while we eat,* she said to herself.

But when she went into the cabin with Bill, there was no sign of Huten. Or of Carey. Barbara placed some huckleberry bread and coffee in front of Amy. Amy wondered whether the others were going to appear and hesitated before starting.

"You go ahead and eat," said Barbara. "Breakfast is pretty casual around here. Huten likes to wait a while before he eats. And Carey likes to sleep late."

There was no option, Amy realized. She was just going to have to start doing her own thing and working with Mercury by herself. Huten wasn't going to come and tell her what to do right away.

She ate the delicious bread slowly. Swallowing the last mouthful of coffee, she thanked Barbara and headed back to the yard. She saddled up Mercury and led him out in the morning sun to the training ring. It was empty. There was no sign of either Bill or Huten. She let Mercury in and began warming him up. He was fresh and skittish from doing no work the day before, and she took her time getting him to calm down and listen to her properly. When he was relaxed, she worked some easy figure eights, enjoying the smooth rhythm of the horse's stride. As she moved him from a trot to a canter, she saw Huten walking down the track toward the training ring.

"Come on, boy," she murmured to Mercury. "You've got an audience."

Mercury arched his neck and lengthened his stride. Amy smiled to herself. It was as though he understood what she had said. He was a true performer. She could well imagine that he had once loved the excitement of the show ring.

After a few more circuits of the ring, Amy heard Huten calling her. She reined Mercury in and trotted over, feeling expectant.

Huten gave her a little smile. "Looks like he's done enough," he said.

Amy was disappointed and surprised. "But I haven't been out here long," she said. "We just finished warming up. He hasn't had much work."

"Take him to the turnout paddock farther down the track," said Huten. "Give him a few hours in the sun."

Slightly baffled, Amy rode Mercury to the gate and dismounted. Huten opened the gate for her, then walked with her back up the track.

"He goes so well in every other way," Amy began to explain. "And he's such a show-off. He must have loved jumping when he first started. I've been trying to find ways to help him rediscover that, but he doesn't seem to want to."

Huten nodded and said nothing for a few minutes. Amy waited, hoping he'd say something perceptive about her riding or her approach.

"He'll enjoy a bit of free time with the other horses," he said eventually.

At this, Amy felt tongue-tied. What did the turnout

paddock have to do with curing his jumping problem? They reached the yard, and she replaced Mercury's saddle and bridle with a halter. As she led him back down the track to the paddock, she decided that she couldn't understand Huten at all. None of what he said was making any sense.

Today, the turnout paddock had three other horses in it. Mercury craned his neck eagerly toward them as Amy opened the gate. She slipped his halter off, and he galloped away with a high-pitched squeal, giving a playful buck as he went. Amy watched him, wishing she felt so carefree. She felt tears pricking at the back of her eyes and blinked them away. *Don't be stupid*, she told herself fiercely. But she couldn't deny what she was feeling — lonely, and homesick for Heartland. This trip was turning out to be very different from what she'd expected.

After lunch, Amy tackled some of her schoolwork. She found it hard to concentrate but forced herself to work for a couple of hours. Then she put her books away and wandered onto the yard. She felt at a loss to know what to do, so she looked for Bill.

"There's not too much work left," said Bill when she asked him. "I'm taking a few people out on a trail ride for the afternoon. A couple of horses need grooming, but I'll have time to do that when I get back. We're not very busy right now."

"Could I groom the horses for you?" asked Amy.

Bill shrugged and smiled. "Sure, if you really want to," he said. "But you don't have to. You can just make yourself at home. You know, chill out."

Amy smiled at Bill's use of the expression. "I'd love to groom," said Amy genuinely. "Just point me in the right direction."

Bill told her where to find Ruby, a chestnut mare, and Mushroom, the roan that she'd seen with Huten the day before.

"Make myself at home?" Amy muttered to herself as she set to work on Ruby with a body brush. "At Heartland, I never have enough time to get everything done, but at least I know what I should be doing." She worked vigorously, raising dust from the mare's back. The rhythm of the work soothed her, and she began to lose herself. She finished with some T-touch circles, enjoying the feeling of Ruby's muscles relaxing beneath her fingers.

After grooming Mushroom, Amy was taking the grooming kit back to the tack room when she saw Huten coming out of one of the stalls with an empty bucket. He raised a hand in greeting. Amy hurried forward eagerly.

"Hi, Huten," she greeted him. "I was thinking of getting Mercury from the paddock and doing another quick session with him. He's been out there a while now. Do you have half an hour to spare?"

Huten smiled slowly and cocked his head to one side.

"Why don't you just head down to the paddock and spend a bit of time with him there," he said. "He'll appreciate that."

And he walked across the yard with the bucket to the faucet. Amy followed him, puzzled.

"What do you mean?" she asked. "Just . . . hang around in the paddock? Don't you think I should work with him some more?"

Huten bent down to turn on the tap and didn't speak until the bucket was full of water. Then he straightened.

"We never stop working here," he said. "But then again, some people might say we never start."

Amy watched him walk slowly back across the yard with the bucket, feeling baffled. She wandered down to the paddock and let herself through the gate. Mercury was grazing peacefully near the three other horses, and Amy walked slowly in their direction. Mercury raised his head and whinnied in greeting. She stopped near him and held out her hand. The gelding came up to her and breathed softly on her fingers. She reached and scratched his forehead as he sniffed around for mints. Finding none, he bent his head to graze again.

"Oh, Mercury," said Amy softly, "I wish I understood you."

The gelding raised his head again and nudged her gently before moving to a patch of grass beyond her. Amy wandered around after him as he grazed from patch to patch, feeling uncertain. Suddenly, misery overcame her. She rested her arms over his withers and buried her head against them. Mercury raised his head in query, then went back to grazing. Amy leaned her forehead against his back as tears flowed down her cheeks, and she played with his mane with her fingers.

After a few minutes, she began to feel better. She straightened up and looked around at the gate. To her horror, Carey was standing there, watching her. Amy hastily wiped her cheeks with her sleeve. How long had she been there, she wondered. But Carey's expression gave nothing away. She just turned and ambled away from the paddock.

Embarrassed, Amy got Mercury's halter and led him back up to the yard. There was no sign of Carey. The shadow of the mountain was beginning to lengthen across the track, and Amy realized she was hungry. She settled Mercury in his stall and headed for the cabin.

As Amy came in, Carey was sprawled on a sofa reading. She yawned and got to her feet. "Good day?" she asked Amy.

Amy felt like saying, *No, I haven't had a good day, and you know I haven't because you saw me in the paddock. I don't know what I'm doing here, and I think I might be wasting my time.* She stared at Carey for a minute. Then she nodded and tried to smile. "Fine, thanks," she said.

She followed Carey through to the kitchen, and they sat down at the table. Soon, Bill and Huten joined them.

"I hope you're all hungry," said Barbara cheerfully. "I was in town for most of the day so I thought I'd get pizza. There was a special — two for one."

"Barbara works part-time," explained Bill to Amy. "She helps run a housing project."

"Not the sort of thing the tourists come to see," added Carey.

Amy noticed Bill and Barbara exchange looks at Carey's words. The looks were sad and resigned. Carey clearly had a thing about Ocanumba being a tourist attraction. And by the looks around the table, it wasn't the first time she had voiced her views on the subject. Amy looked at Huten. He was nodding to himself.

"People see what they want to see," he said. "Wherever they are."

Chapter Seven

After breakfast the next morning, Amy found Huten waiting for her on the yard.

"We're taking a walk," he announced.

"Oh, OK," said Amy. "Shall I saddle Mercury?"

"No, no," said Huten. "I mean on foot."

Amy was beginning to see that there was little point in questioning the way things happened around here. "OK," she said. "Where are we going?"

"Through the forest," said Huten. "You won't need anything," he added, anticipating her thoughts. She'd been wondering whether to go back for her coat.

Huten set off on a trail that led down the mountainside. Amy followed behind him, trying not to worry about where he was taking her. As they walked, she took in the fresh smell of leaves and the creaking of branches.

After about an hour, they emerged onto a wider path, and Amy could see buildings ahead. It looked like a good-sized village. The trail led down between some houses and emerged onto a paved road.

The village was much busier than it had looked from the mountainside above. Amy spotted two tourist buses and people wandering around, carrying cameras. She and Huten walked past numerous craft workshops. Some of them belonged to Native American artisans, and Amy took a look at the beautiful carvings, ceramics, and baskets on sale. In one shop, there were demonstrations for the tourists of how the old craft traditions were being kept alive. She was tempted to pause, but Huten quickly took her off the main road again and led her on a paved path to a small workshop at the edge of the village.

Inside sat a man who looked about Huten's age. He was bent over a half-finished basket, methodically weaving the reeds in and out of the struts rising up from the bottom. Huten entered the workshop and beckoned Amy to do the same.

The man acknowledged Huten with a brief nod of his head, but he didn't stop working. Huten sat on the floor and indicated the spot next to him. "Sit," he instructed Amy.

Amy sat down and crossed her legs. Huten sat silently, watching the basket weaver. Amy did the same, fascinated by the swift and delicate movements of the man's hands.

After about twenty minutes, Huten leaned to one side and reached for the pile of finished baskets piled up behind the basket weaver. He lifted the top one and placed it in front of him. Then he reached for one of the reeds sitting in a neat pile next to the weaver.

Amy was curious. Huten regarded her and smiled slowly. "When you watch the basket weaver at work," he asked, "what is he concentrating on? The reed? Or the finished basket?"

Amy looked back at the weaver. As she watched, he deftly secured the end of one reed and reached for the next. She thought how he must have the finished basket in his mind's eye the whole time.

She turned back to Huten. "The finished basket," she answered.

"Well . . . I can see why you said that," he responded with a knowing smile.

He said nothing more. Amy wasn't sure whether she'd given the right answer or not, but it was clear that the lesson was over.

Huten then took her to an area of slightly elevated land beyond the village. From there, it was possible to see the main buildings at its center. They were crowded with visitors taking pictures of one another. Amy was reminded of Carey's words, but it was clear that the village was being kept alive by tourists' money. Although everything was changing all the while, the tourism was maintaining the time-honored craft methods and supporting the craftspeople. Amy was touched that Huten wanted to show her this. She felt that she was seeing something precious from the inside. But at the back of her mind, a voice kept whispering, *What about Mercury? When will we ever deal with him?*

Huten turned onto the trail once more, and they were soon climbing back the way they'd come. The sun was hot, and Amy felt herself breaking into a sweat. Huten, however, seemed unaffected. He walked at the same even pace until they reached the yard again.

Once there, Huten disappeared into his own part of the cabin. Amy was thirsty and went in search of something cold to drink. Stepping into the kitchen, she found Barbara and Carey sitting at the table. They were speaking in their dialect.

As soon as Amy came in, Barbara smiled, and they switched to English.

"Don't stop for me!" exclaimed Amy. "I'd love to hear you speak your language."

"Oh, we can't do that," said Barbara. "It would be rude."

"Please," said Amy. "I've never heard it before. Don't

worry about me. I'd just like something cold to drink, if that's OK."

Barbara smiled and indicated the fridge. "Help yourself," she said. Then, after a moment's hesitation, she addressed Carey in their own tongue again. Carey laughed and said something in reply.

Amy poured herself a glass of apple juice and sat at the table with them, listening in fascination. She watched Carey's face and thought how lively it seemed. *How odd,* she thought to herself. *Carey claims to want to move away, but she looks so much more at ease when she speaks her own language.*

❧

Amy heard the clatter of hooves on the yard as she went to check on Mercury later in the afternoon. Bill was leading Ruby in the direction of the training ring.

"Are you working with Ruby for a while?" Amy asked.

"Yes," said Bill, "but there's plenty of room in the ring for two of us to work."

"That's OK," said Amy. "I think I'll go for a ride on the trails instead."

She went to get Mercury's tack and decided to ask Huten for some suggestions for a good trail ride. She found him grooming in one of the stalls. He came out to point her in the right direction.

"Head up that trail," he said. "Follow it until you come

to a signpost. Take the second path to the right — that'll bring you back to the stables by a quicker route."

"Thanks, Huten," said Amy, turning Mercury toward the forest.

Soon she was completely surrounded by trees. Mercury walked forward with his ears pricked, eagerly sizing up his new surroundings, and, in places where the trail widened out, Amy nudged him into a trot. His stride was relaxed and happy. *At least he's having a good time*, Amy reflected.

But Amy knew Mercury wasn't here just to have a good time. She wished she had some idea of where things were going. She hadn't even discussed Mercury's jumping problem with Huten. And, she realized with a pang, Mercury might be having a good time, but she certainly wasn't. She was feeling confused, and she missed everyone at home. If only Ty were near so that she could discuss everything with him. She hadn't expected to feel so homesick.

As she came out of her reverie, she realized that the shadows were beginning to lengthen and the sun was dropping lower between the trees. Then, in front of her, appeared a fork. *Take the second path*, Huten had said. She looked around her. She couldn't see a signpost, but she couldn't believe that the trail continued much farther. Huten knew that she didn't have much time before sundown — he wouldn't have sent her out on a long ride. Had she missed the signpost farther back? She couldn't be sure.

She could see that just down the right-hand path there was a fork, too. It made sense for that to be the second path. She hesitated. The light was beginning to fade, and Huten had said that the second path was a quicker route. She could just turn back the way she'd come, but she must have been riding for nearly an hour. It would be completely dark by the time she got back if she did that.

She wondered what to do. She thought back. She couldn't remember seeing any other tracks. This must be the turning that Huten had told her about. Quickly, she made a decision and turned Mercury down the right-hand path. Then she took the second path that forked off it. That would basically take her in a circle, she reasoned — and back to the stables. She nudged Mercury into a trot.

But after about twenty minutes, the trail seemed to turn back on itself. Amy reined Mercury in. This wasn't right. If the trail led back to the stables by a short route, she should be nearing them by now. The sun had disappeared, and dusk was setting in. Twenty minutes more and it would be dark.

Amy swallowed and squeezed Mercury on again. Fear began to grip her. The path wound between the trees, still climbing uphill. Amy knew from the way she'd come that she should be going downhill by now. *This doesn't make sense,* she kept saying to herself. *But I can't be lost. I can't be lost. The stables must appear soon.*

But as the darkness grew deeper, Amy knew that however many times she said it, it didn't make any difference. She was lost. Completely and utterly lost.

Chapter Eight

"Is anyone there?" Amy called into the darkness. There was no response.

"Hello!" she hollered, hearing the fear in her own voice. The darkness was developing a thick, velvet coat, and the woods were strangely silent. She stopped Mercury again and sat, a pit in the bottom of her stomach. What should she do? If she was going the wrong way, it would be crazy to keep going. But if she retraced her path, she would be riding for another hour and a half or longer, and she might even take a wrong path in the darkness. Mercury snorted, twitching his ears. Amy stared into the darkness, thinking furiously.

She'd been lost once before — in the woods back home. Star, the horse she'd been riding then, had found his own way back. Could Mercury possibly find his way back now, she wondered? He didn't know the area, and they weren't even on the same trail they'd taken into the forest. But his senses were much stronger than hers. He might be able to pick out clues about their direction that she couldn't detect.

It was her only option. She let the reins drop on Mercury's neck and gently urged him forward. Mercury didn't hesitate. He started to walk purposefully forward, following the same track that they'd been on for the last forty minutes or so. Amy felt helpless, but Mercury's ears were pricked. He knew he was going somewhere, that was clear. She let him continue on.

As Mercury's stride quickened, Amy had a sudden thought. Had Huten been working with her all along, when she'd been assuming he hadn't? Was this ride into the forest part of it? He seemed to have been saying something about letting things take their own course and reveal themselves naturally. Was he saying this about Mercury? She wasn't sure, but perhaps she'd been looking at things the wrong way.

She snapped out of her thoughts to realize that the night air was growing colder. Whatever Huten was trying to tell her, the fact was that she still didn't know where she was, she thought despairingly. The trees seemed to be darker and closer. The only consolation was that the trail had at last started to dip down, and Mercury's ears were still pricked forward. Amy closed her eyes for a few moments and fought the panic that was rising once more.

Suddenly, Amy thought she heard something. She pulled Mercury up, her heart pounding. But there was nothing. Silence. She nudged Mercury on again. He responded willingly, his step springy as he rounded a twist in the trail. Amy caught a glimpse of something ahead and craned her neck. It disappeared again. Could it be? They rounded another bend, and this time there was no doubt. There were lights ahead, the comforting lights of the stables, with the cabin lights twinkling behind. She heaved a sigh of relief. "Good boy, Mercury," she whispered.

To her surprise, there was no one waiting anxiously for her on the yard. She dismounted and led Mercury to his stall. As she lifted the saddle from his back, she realized that her legs were trembling. She put the saddle over the half door and flung her arms around Mercury's neck, burying her face in his mane. *I was really, really scared out there,* she thought. *And if this was Heartland, they'd have sent out a search party by now.* A sob escaped her and as it did, she heard a noise at the stable door. She looked up and saw Huten regarding her gently.

"You're back," he said with a nod.

Amy felt speechless. She opened her mouth angrily, but nothing came out. Huten said nothing more but stood there, simply looking at her with that inscrutable smile. Then he moved away from the doorway, leaving Amy on her own with Mercury.

When he had gone, Amy felt rage rising inside her. How could he be so unconcerned? What was going on here? Had she come all this way to be neglected? Maybe Ty was right; it seemed like a wild-goose chase. Maybe Marion had gotten it wrong about Huten and his family. Amy had learned over the last few months that her mother may have been wonderful, but she wasn't perfect. Perhaps now Amy was paying the price for being so sure about her mother's instincts. Amy had wanted to know for herself what her mother had discovered from Huten, but maybe it wasn't meant for her to learn.

She stomped to the tack room with Mercury's tack, then headed indoors. The family hadn't eaten supper yet — in fact it looked as though they'd been waiting for her. But no one said anything about her ride or the fact that it was late and dark. As she came in, Barbara gave her a welcoming smile as though nothing out of the ordinary had happened. Huten was his usual quiet, reflective self at the dinner table. Even Bill was silent. Only Carey raised an eyebrow, but like the others, she said nothing.

Amy took her place at the table, and Barbara served up a steaming pot roast. Amy didn't feel like eating much. She felt lost and alone and — she had to admit to herself — frightened, even back in the safety of the cabin.

🙠

After supper she went to her room and picked up her cell phone. She dialed Ty's number. It seemed to ring forever, and she willed him to pick it up. At that point there was no one in the world she wanted to talk to more.

To her relief, after four more rings he answered.

"Ty, it's me — Amy," she said, slightly nervously.

"Amy!" exclaimed Ty. "It's good to hear your voice."

"And yours," said Amy with feeling.

"So how's it going?" asked Ty. "Is Mercury making progress?"

Amy felt a tide of shame wash over her. Words began to spill out. "Ty, I don't know what's going on. I think maybe you were right, I shouldn't have come. Nothing makes any sense, we haven't even done any real work with Mercury. Huten doesn't say much at all. I think maybe he's trying to get me to look at things in a different way. But then this afternoon he sent me out on this trail ride into the forest, and I got completely lost. I had to let Mercury find the way back for me. By then it was completely dark. I was so scared, Ty. But the family doesn't seem to be the slightest bit bothered about it. It's almost like they knew it would happen . . . and . . . and . . . Ty, I miss you." Amy paused. "And I'm really sorry," she finished in a broken voice. "I'm really sorry everything was so difficult before I left, and I'm really sorry I was so stubborn about Mercury."

There was a brief silence at the other end of the phone. Amy waited anxiously, not knowing how he would respond.

When he spoke, Ty's voice was warm and gentle. "Amy," he said softly, "you're being really hard on yourself. You're in a strange place and it takes time to adjust. You don't need to apologize to me. You know I understand what you're going through." He paused, then added, "And you know, I don't think you made the wrong decision. I think you should let things run their course. You knew there wouldn't be an instant fix for Mercury. Things may become clearer by the end of the week. I can't believe that you and Marion were so wrong about Huten."

Amy listened to his words. She should have known that Ty would understand.

"Thanks, Ty," she said. "I hope you're right. I'll let you know how things go over the next few days."

"Sounds good," said Ty. "Take care of yourself."

"Thanks, you too," said Amy.

🙊

Amy put the phone down, filled with relief now that she and Ty were speaking easily to each other again. Still, it hadn't changed the fact that she couldn't see where things were going with Mercury. Feeling restless, she slipped on her coat and headed out of the cabin. It was a clear, still night, and the stars seemed bright and close. Now that she was safe, the darkness had lost its terror.

She walked around the stable block, greeting the horses, who were peering out of their stalls curiously. She stopped at Maverick's stall. She could see the wariness in the pony's eyes as he observed her from the back of the stall.

"Hello, little fella," she said softly. She felt the sudden urge to enter his stall and try to reach him, but just as she put her hand on the bolt, she heard footsteps. She looked around.

It was Carey, approaching her across the yard.

Amy sighed with frustration. Whenever she thought she was alone, someone unexpectedly showed up. She didn't know how she felt about any of them. She wasn't sure if she could trust them.

"I heard you leave the cabin," Carey said as she came up to Amy.

Amy regarded the other girl cautiously. "I wanted a bit of fresh air," she said. "I guess I need to think things over."

"Are you OK?" Carey asked bluntly. Carey looked embarrassed and awkward. "I mean, you don't look like you are."

Amy hesitated. Carey hadn't given much indication before that she wanted to be friendly. "I was really scared in the forest," she admitted.

Carey shrugged. "Granddad's got a funny way of doing things," she said.

"What do you mean?" Amy asked, her anger returning. "I don't think it was very funny. All I know is that I got lost and no one seemed to care."

Carey gave a little smile. "You can't get lost in that part of the forest," she said. "Or not for long, anyway. All the paths come back to the stables eventually, because none of them lead over the mountain. It's true that they zigzag around a bit first. If you're lost, it's just a matter of luck whether you find a path that leads back quickly."

"But Huten told me which one to take," protested Amy.

"Probably the second one," guessed Carey.

"Yes," said Amy, her confusion growing. "But I must have missed it. He said there was a signpost, but I didn't see one."

"It's easy to miss," said Carey. "But Granddad knew you'd come back safely."

"How do you know for sure?" asked Amy angrily.

Carey regarded her expression calmly. "Look, I saw you looking pretty upset in the paddock yesterday. You're really not finding this easy, are you?" she asked in a quiet voice.

"Finding what easy?" exclaimed Amy. "As far as I can tell, not a lot has been happening. We haven't worked with Mercury at all. This isn't the way I expected it to be."

"Life often isn't," commented Carey.

Amy shrugged, her anger ebbing away. She looked again into Maverick's stall. He was still standing at the back looking tense.

"Why don't you go in?" asked Carey suddenly. "I could tell you wanted to when I came from the cabin."

Amy hesitated. She looked at the wild-eyed pony again. "I'd like to see if I can reach him, you know, help him to relax around me," she said.

She quietly slid back the bolt and let herself into the stall. Carey slipped in after her. Maverick snorted, shifting nervously around the back of his stall. Amy extended her hand slowly.

"Come on, boy," she breathed. "There's nothing to be afraid of."

Tentatively, Maverick stretched his neck out and sniffed her hand.

"He's getting a lot better at tolerating people in his stall," said Carey. "When he first came, we couldn't get anywhere near him."

Amy looked at her quickly. What did she mean, *we*? She'd told Amy that she didn't work with the horses. But as Carey stepped forward and approached Maverick slowly, it was clear that he was familiar with her. Either that, or her presence was naturally soothing. Maverick seemed to calm down, and Carey placed her hand gently on his neck. She stroked him softly for a few minutes, then began to work up his neck in gentle circling motions with her fingers.

Amy watched in astonishment. "You use T-touch," she said in a low voice.

Carey gave her a blank look. "I use what?" she asked.

Amy motioned to Carey's hand on Maverick's neck. "T-touch. What you're doing on his neck — the massage technique."

Carey shrugged. "I didn't know it had a name," she said. "It's just the way I've always tried to calm horses."

She's a natural, Amy thought to herself. She was moved and impressed. She watched as Maverick began to relax under the calming influence of Carey's fingers.

"I just don't get it," Amy said to Carey suddenly. "You say you want to get away from your roots. How can you say that when the life here is so much a part of you?"

Carey looked at her in surprise. "A part of me?" she asked.

"Yes," said Amy. "Look at you. You have a natural touch with horses. Don't pretend you don't. I think you understand your Granddad's work, too, no matter what you say."

Carey reached Maverick's ears and made tiny circles with her fingers around his forelock. Maverick snorted in appreciation. But when she looked up at Amy, she was frowning. "That doesn't mean I feel the life here is right for me," she said. "I'm not all that excited about inheriting the family horse business, OK? What would you know about it? It's just not what I want right now."

Amy leaned against the stall partition and regarded Carey coolly. "Sometimes what you want isn't what you need," she said, feeling slightly put off by Carey's attitude. "You're so lucky to have Huten. I'd give anything to have my Mom back, to be able to work with her again. That's not going to happen. But I am happy that I learned what I could from her in the time we had. I learned about so much more than the family horse business."

"Well, I can see your point," Carey said. "But with your mom and all, it's different for you. I know a lot of people linger in the past because they don't want to risk forgetting what they had. But for me, I still feel that it's better to look forward. To find my own path."

"Maybe you don't have to do just one or the other," said Amy. "Maybe you can move forward and not let go of the past."

Maverick, now completely relaxed, butted Carey with his muzzle. Carey stepped back and folded her arms. She nodded slowly. "Well," she said, "maybe you're right. You have an interesting way of seeing things. I'm sure you'll soon figure out what Granddad is trying to show you."

Amy was curious. "So, wait. You know what he's doing?" she asked.

Carey looked at her strangely. "Yes. You'll find out, too, soon enough," she said.

Chapter Nine

A twig snapped under Amy's feet, breaking the silence of the forest. Huten was ahead of her, walking silently. Amy felt clumsy as she followed after him, her footsteps seeming heavy and intrusive in comparison with his.

It was the next morning, and Huten had told her that they were going for a walk in the forest. They paced along in silence as the morning sun glinted on bright drops of dew caught on spiderwebs and the fresh green leaves of the trees.

Amy felt more settled now. Talking to Ty had made her feel that perhaps things were going to work out after all. And in an odd way, the chat with Carey had helped, too. She had to be patient.

Soon she heard the sound of water ahead. It grew louder, and suddenly there it was — a gushing trout stream making its way over and around pebbles and boulders. Huten walked upstream for a while until they reached a flat boulder overhanging the stream. He squatted down, and Amy sat next to him. They watched the water gurgling past.

After a moment, Huten turned to her.

"The stream doesn't know where it has come from," he said. "Or where it's going."

Amy listened and nodded.

"We like to think we know where our path leads," Huten continued. "And where we are from. But nature doesn't think this way. It does what it does for its own reasons."

Amy spotted the quicksilver flash of a trout as it snatched a fly off the surface of the stream.

Huten smiled. "Perhaps one day the stream will turn on its tail and flow backward," he said.

Amy smiled, too. Then Huten stood suddenly and stepped back into the forest. Amy was taken by surprise and scrambled to follow him. But by the time she was on her feet, he had already disappeared, swallowed up by the dark spaces between the trees.

She sat back down on the boulder. She was getting used to Huten. She guessed that he meant for her to stay for as long as she wanted and find her own way back. She thought of Carey's words. "The point is that you find out for yourself." Carey obviously knew that there was more to this week than she'd realized. Huten wasn't ignoring the issue of Mercury at all.

Amy reflected on the trip that they'd made down to the village. She remembered the weaver's hands, concentrating methodically — not on the finished basket, she realized suddenly, but on each individual reed. Something was beginning to make sense. She thought of the way she had been viewing Mercury. Because he was such a performer, such a competitor, she'd been focusing on the end result. It was easy to picture Mercury sailing around the showring, responding to the excitement and the praise. She stared into the stream. *The stream doesn't know where it has come from,* she heard Huten say again. *Or where it's going.*

She and Ben had been approaching Mercury so logically. They could see that he was born to compete. But Mercury couldn't understand how his temperament was linked to jumping. He didn't know what they were trying to achieve with him. All he knew was that he no longer wanted to jump fences, because it wasn't fun. It didn't feel like a natural challenge anymore.

Amy stood up and started making her way back through the forest. After what Carey had told her, she was no longer afraid of getting lost. She let her instincts guide her. Here and there she saw clues left by herself and Huten on their way up — a snapped twig or the faint imprint of a foot on the soft floor of the forest — and knew that she was heading the right way.

She thought back to how sure Mercury had been when she'd left him to his own devices in the dark. *The second path,* she thought, and smiled. The second path had turned out to be the one she and Mercury had figured out for themselves. The second path was found by trusting your instincts.

And that's it, she concluded, feeling suddenly excited. *Mercury has to rediscover jumping on his own terms, not on the terms that we lay down for him.* There weren't any perfect solutions or outcomes. Sometimes you had to let the best solution reveal itself little by little.

She came upon the stables again quicker than she expected and rushed to find Huten. She was dying to tell him what she'd worked out.

She found him in the training ring with Maverick. Amy stood at the gate, not wanting to disturb Huten's work. It was clear that Huten, like Carey, had gained the half mustang's trust. He was slowly working toward breaking him in. But as with Albatross, he wasn't working with anything that might control the horse, like a bridle or saddle. It was just himself and Maverick in the ring.

Amy watched intently as the old man laid his hand on the horse's back and gently applied some pressure. Maverick turned his head inquiringly but didn't move. Huten slid his arm farther across his back and pressed a little harder. As he did so, he saw Amy at the gate and raised his other hand. Then he returned his concentration to Maverick and didn't come over until the session had finished. Huten could now place his entire weight on the mustang's back without him trying to move away.

"So how's it going?" asked Huten as he opened the gate.

"Good," said Amy, the words tumbling out of her. "I think I've worked out what you were trying to say. About the basket weaver and the stream and everything else. Even about getting lost in the forest. They were all part of the same lesson. I think I know how to work with Mercury now. . . ." she trailed off when she saw Huten's face. He had barely raised an eyebrow.

She grinned at him. "I understand," she said simply.

"Come on, boy," she said to Mercury later that day. "We're going to do something different."

She saddled him up and rode down to the training ring, where she had already set up a few small jumps at one end. Mercury eyed them suspiciously, as though they were monsters. Amy ignored his reaction and warmed him up at the other end of the ring. Then she rode him down in between the jumps. Straightaway, he became nervous and tense. But Amy simply brought him to a halt near a low vertical, then let the reins relax. She didn't give him any other aids at all and sat quite still in the saddle.

At first, Mercury stood where he was, as though he was waiting for Amy to tell him what to do next. Then he looked around inquiringly.

"It's OK, boy," said Amy in a soft voice. "It's up to you."

Mercury seemed bewildered. He stretched his neck out low toward the ground and snorted. Then he took a few wandering steps forward. He reached out to sniff at the upright, and as his nose touched it, his body shuddered and shot back. Amy sat easily and stroked his neck.

"Take it easy," she murmured.

Mercury sniffed curiously at the upright again, and this time he didn't recoil. He nosed the wood for a minute or two, then seemed to lose interest. He turned toward the other end of the ring and quietly ambled away from the jumps.

Amy stroked his neck and talked to him, then took up the reins again and did some more schooling work before taking him back to his stall. Amy couldn't be sure if his experience of sniffing at the jumps was the first step toward acceptance. It was hard to say. But something told Amy she was heading in the right direction.

❧

The next morning, Amy watched Huten with Maverick again. With every day that passed, the half mustang was giving Huten more of his trust, letting himself relax a little bit more, a sign of gratitude to someone who had shown he wouldn't hurt him. It reminded Amy of join up, the technique she often used at Heartland. It was a way of bonding with a horse and establishing trust. In the course of join up, a horse began to want to be with you and made that choice freely. In a similar way, Maverick was beginning to crave Huten's company. He was happy to put up with Huten's weight on his back if it meant he was able to stay with him.

As Amy watched, she pondered the next step with Mercury. The important thing, she realized, was to concentrate on what Mercury *wanted* to do, not what he didn't want to do. And a good place to start would be with join up.

When the training ring was free, Amy went to get the gelding. She unclipped the lead rope from his halter and drove him away from her, around the ring. As usual, he spooked at the low jumps that were still set up at one end. He stuck to trotting in a small circle in the half ring that was set off by the fences. When he was as far away from the jumps as possible, he slowed to a walk and looked at Amy inquiringly. She turned her shoulders square to his and looked at him sternly, driving him back into a trot. She was showing him that he couldn't stop working as easily as that.

Mercury started away from her and broke into a canter, again carefully avoiding getting too close to the jumps. He slowed to a trot, and Amy drove him on again, not letting him rest for a minute. When he had been forced around the ring several times at a fast trot, Amy began to see the signs she was looking for. First, Mercury's inside ear began to twitch in her direction. It wasn't long before he started lowering his head and making chewing movements with his lips. This was Mercury's signal that he didn't want to be driven around the edge of the ring anymore, where he was forced to work on his own. He wanted to be with Amy instead, in the middle of the ring.

Amy was always thrilled when a horse reached this point. However many times it happened, it still seemed like a miracle. She changed her aggressive posture, letting her shoulders sag, and turned her back on Mercury. She heard him slow to a walk, then a halt. He seemed to hesitate. Then she heard the sound of his hooves on the sand, approaching her. Soon his warm breath was blowing down her neck as he nuzzled her shoulder.

She turned around slowly and stroked his nose. "Good boy," she murmured in delight.

Then she adopted the aggressive posture again, driving Mercury away from her. Mercury jumped back in bewilderment and trotted away anxiously. Amy knew that once a horse had reached this stage, he would want to come into the center again very quickly. The connection with her was what he craved.

So as he began to lower his head and chew once more, Amy turned her back and waited for Mercury to join her again. This time, it happened almost immediately. Amy walked around the ring, with him following behind. Whichever way she turned, Mercury kept up with her, his muzzle right at her shoulder.

Amy walked closer to the jumps, wondering how Mercury would respond. Yesterday, he'd made up his mind that they weren't anything to worry about — as long as he wasn't asked to jump them. Now, Amy wasn't even riding him, but he was still aware of them. Even as he followed her as she walked around, he seemed to eye the jumps suspiciously. But he didn't leave her side. Amy wondered how deep his trust in her was. How important was it for him to be with her.

Spontaneously, Amy broke into a jog and hopped right over one of the jumps herself. Mercury was taken by surprise and stood still looking at her. Amy returned his gaze. The quickest way for him to join her again would be to jump the little fence. Did he trust her enough to follow her example? She held her breath. He was free to veer around the side, if he wanted to. Or would he not follow her at all?

It took only a second for Mercury to decide. With his ears pricked forward, he broke into a trot. With a flick of his tail, he bounced over the jump and joined Amy on the other side.

Amy wanted to leap around in delight but knew she must reinforce Mercury's trust by staying calm. So instead, she put her arms around the gelding's neck and rubbed his mane.

"You're such a good boy, Mercury," she said, her heart fizzing. "Such a wonderfully good boy."

Chapter Ten

Amy looked up and noticed two figures watching her from the side of the ring — Huten and Carey.

"Hey!" she called. She saw that Carey was looking impressed. Amy grinned and led Mercury over to the fence. Huten said nothing, but there was warmth in his eyes — and understanding. It was all Amy needed. She smiled at him.

"He chose to jump," she said happily. "He wanted to."

"It's amazing," said Carey, disbelief in her voice. "We were watching him. But it was like he hardly saw the jump — he was totally thinking about getting back to you."

Amy hugged Mercury again. He snorted and arched his neck, enjoying the attention.

"Come on, boy," she said to him. "You've done enough for one day. How about a few hours in the pasture?"

But before leading Mercury to the gate, she looked at her mentor. "Huten," she said quietly, "you've shown me a different way of looking at things. Thank you."

"You found that path for yourself," said Huten. He smiled slowly. "A teacher must learn to become invisible," he added softly. "And must understand that power in all its forms."

Amy listened, feeling slightly puzzled. She wondered if his words made any more sense to Carey. To her surprise, the older girl had tears in her eyes. When she realized that Amy was looking at her, she blinked them quickly away.

"Granddad's right," she said quietly. "You've found your own way. That's pretty special, Amy."

Amy pondered Huten's mysterious words as she led Mercury down the track to the turnout paddock. She understood what he meant — that if he had simply taken control and told her what to do, she would have learned very little herself. By seeming to do nothing, he had forced her to rethink things for herself until the solution became evident. And perhaps, in a similar way, she had found a way to reach Mercury by making the jump seem invisible, too.

But there was still a long way to go. Mercury had jumped only one fence. He would have to repeat the exercise many times before he could truly overcome his fear.

❧

Ty's voice sounded warm and close when Amy spoke to him later that day.

"So how are things working out?" asked Ty.

"Not bad, actually," said Amy. She paused, then announced, "Mercury jumped for the first time today."

"Oh, wow! Tell me how it happened!" Ty demanded.

Amy explained about using join up, and how Mercury had hardly seemed to care about the jump.

"I am so proud of you," said Ty, when she'd finished. "And Mercury, of course."

Amy felt touched and warmed by his words. Ty was so generous — he was so willing to admit when he thought he was in the wrong. But a pang of guilt went through her as she realized he was being far too generous this time.

"Ty, it wasn't me who was right," she said. "It was you. You thought that Ben and I were wrong to be concentrating so much on the jumping."

"Yes, but you were sure we could find a way around it," said Ty. "You knew Mercury's personality."

Amy smiled to herself at his words. "But I didn't think I was getting anywhere here. You told me to be patient and see what happened," she said.

"OK, OK," laughed Ty. "It was a joint effort. Can we agree on that?"

"It's a deal," Amy agreed happily. Then she paused and said, "I miss you, Ty. And I realize that something Huten said has made me think about us, too. I've been trying to figure out where we're going. I want to know how it will all work out in the end. But what I've learned with Mercury is that you just have to trust yourself and let things work themselves out. Maybe that's what I should do with us." Amy paused, a little surprised at herself. "Ty," she continued, "I just want to say I'm sorry."

"Amy, you don't need to be sorry," said Ty gently. "It's not easy when you start going out with one of your best friends, but I know it's worth it. And you're right. We should just trust each other and let things work themselves out."

❧

Amy waited for the soft thud of Mercury's hooves on the sand as he cleared the fence once more. It was Thursday, two days since he'd jumped for the first time. Amy had repeated the experiment each day, changing or raising the fences slightly every time. The changes made no difference to Mercury. He jumped them all easily, eager to demonstrate his trust and to be with Amy.

Each time Amy and Mercury did a session, Carey came and watched. She seemed fascinated, and her distant air gradually disappeared. "When are you going to try riding him?" she called from the ringside, when Mercury was happily nuzzling Amy's shoulder. Amy led him over to the fence.

"Not today," said Amy. "But I'd like to before I leave. I guess that means tomorrow. My last day. Ty's coming to pick me up on Saturday morning."

"Your last day," Carey repeated. A look of disappointment flickered across her face, but it faded quickly. "So you're not working him again today?" she asked.

Amy looked up at Mercury's relaxed, alert face. "No. I don't want to rush him. Why?"

Carey hesitated. "Would you like to go for a trail ride with me this afternoon then?"

Amy was surprised and pleased. "I'd like that," she said.

"Good," said Carey. "There's something I want to show you."

❧

They rode out of the stables after lunch, Carey on Sandy and Amy on Mercury. They took a trail that led in a direction Amy hadn't been before, leading away from the cabin. It looked as though it might lead right around the mountain, but Amy remembered what Carey had told her — none of the trails did that. They rode in silence for a while, the sun hot on the backs of their necks. It was the first time Amy had seen Carey ride, and she had the same graceful ease as Huten. Even though Sandy was tacked up, Carey still managed to look as though she was part of the horse's back.

"I don't understand why you don't ride more," said Amy after a while. "You're such a natural."

Carey smiled and gave Amy a mysterious look. "Well, maybe I'll be riding a bit more from now on."

"Really?" asked Amy. "But what about your plans?"

Carey shrugged. "My plans weren't so hot." She grinned as they reached an open clearing in the woods. "Come on, let's get moving," she said, giving Sandy her head. The mare surged forward eagerly, and Mercury followed, right on her heels. They rode the trail as it wound through the trees, climbing slightly. As they rounded a bend, Carey slowed Sandy to a trot, and Amy suddenly heard the sound of gushing water.

Carey turned in her saddle. "This is my place," she said. "I kind of think of it as mine, anyway. No one else comes here."

They rode forward between slabs of rock. Then, up ahead, a waterfall came into view, cascading down from boulders high above in the forest. Amy stared up at its source, feeling spray settling on her hair and eyebrows. It was only about three feet in width, but with the spring rains, a full torrent was gushing down.

When she looked forward again, her heart stopped.

Carey and Sandy were nowhere to be seen. She pulled Mercury to a halt.

"Carey?" she called. There was no answer, and she rode Mercury forward toward the cascade. The trail beneath Mercury's hooves was much more uneven, and he picked his way carefully. Amy stopped him again. The path looked as though it was going to disappear.

"Hey!" a voice called behind her.

Amy jumped and spun around in her saddle. "Carey!" she exclaimed. "How did you do that? You were just in front of me."

Carey grinned. She swung herself out of her saddle and jerked her head backward. "Let me show you," she said.

Amy dismounted and led Mercury after Carey. As they reached a small bend ahead, Carey seemed to be suddenly engulfed by the rocks to one side. Amy peered forward. Now she could see that the rock formed a dense shadow where it created an overhang and that underneath, there was a big, cavernous opening. Tentatively, she stepped inside and let her eyes adjust to the darkness for a few seconds.

"Wow," she breathed, as shapes began to emerge from the blackness. "What a great place." The cavern had a smooth, sandy floor and moss growing up its sheer sides. Carey was busy tying Sandy's reins to a bracket that had been hammered into the rock.

Carey motioned for Amy to lead Mercury forward. He stepped forward nervously, spooking at the darkness, but Sandy snorted at him reassuringly. Amy tied his halter rope quickly and joined Carey at the other end of the cavern, where she was standing in a small pool of light. Carey pointed up. Far, far above there was a circle of daylight, right where the cavern emerged onto the mountainside.

"The spy hole," she said. "The forest can watch me from up there and make sure I'm not getting into any trouble."

Amy laughed softly. "You said that no one else comes here?"

Carey looked at her coolly and shook her head. "Consider yourself lucky," she said, squatting down on the sandy floor. "I don't bring just anybody here."

Amy squatted down next to her. "Thanks," she said. "I appreciate it."

Carey studied her face in the half-light. "I knew you would," she said. She paused, then gestured around her. "My ancestors used this cave for centuries. You can't see the signs easily, but they're here." She pointed up again.

Amy squinted, unsure what she was pointing at.

"The rock's blackened in places," said Carey.

Amy looked at her inquiringly.

"Fires," said Carey. "This place is part of some of our ancient stories. The old folks think it is a place of wisdom. They call it One Eye."

Amy peered up at the circle of light once again as Carey continued. "I spent hours here on my own when I was younger. I used to imagine the forest talking to me through the Eye. It took me ages to get that bracket into the rock — I used to sneak Dad's tools up here. But that's the only thing I've changed about it. It's not the sort of place that should change."

Amy could feel what she meant. There was something timeless about the muted sound of the waterfall outside and the inky darkness inside the cave.

"When were you last here?" she asked Carey.

Carey was silent for a few minutes, then she said, "I haven't been here for nearly a year. I haven't been here since I first decided I wanted to leave Ten Beeches. I realized I was lonely. There wasn't anyone else my age hanging around, and there was so much talk about holding on to the past. That's when I decided I wanted to go and find a different life somewhere else and forget about this life."

Amy nodded slowly. "So how do you feel now?" she asked.

"Seeing you work with Mercury made me realize how well I understand Granddad's work," said Carey. "I could see you struggling, even though I could follow Granddad's teachings. But it was amazing, seeing your bond with Mercury grow. And you made me appreciate the bond I have with Maverick, too. So I guess I feel like

I should work at what I have here — find ways to make it work for me. I think I still have a lot to learn."

Amy thought of how Lou had given up her job in New York to work at Heartland, and she knew that it hadn't been an easy decision. She guessed that this wasn't easy for Carey, either. "I'm glad," said Amy. "I really am."

"You know, I brought you here because I wanted to thank you," said Carey. "I thought that coming all this way with a horse was a bit crazy, at first. But the way you dealt with Mercury really impressed me, Amy. You fight for what you believe in, and you don't give up. Even when you don't have the answers, you have faith in yourself."

Amy felt moved. "I have to admit, I was about to give up," she said. "You helped me understand what Huten was doing."

"Did I?" asked Carey. "I guess I wasn't sure that I wanted to."

"Well, you did," said Amy. "And I'm grateful for that."

The sound of Mercury stamping a hind hoof on the soft floor of the cave broke into their conversation. Amy laughed.

"I think he's getting bored."

"I guess life revelations aren't so interesting for him," said Carey. "Well, let's get back on the trail."

She scrambled to her feet, and Amy followed. They

untied the horses and led them out into the sunlight, which was dazzling after the dim light of the cave.

Carey led the way back down the trail. As Amy watched Carey's black hair shining in the sunlight, she smiled to herself. She had the feeling that Carey didn't make friends easily. But when she did, she made them for life.

❧

"So today's the big day?" asked Carey at breakfast the next morning, looking at Amy.

"You mean riding Mercury over some jumps?" said Amy. She looked across at Huten and smiled. "Yes, I think it might be."

"You'll have an audience," said Bill. "If that's OK."

"Who?" asked Amy, astonished.

Bill smiled. "All of us, of course," he said. "We think you've done a good week's work. We want to see the results!"

Amy flushed slightly at this praise. She hadn't realized that she'd been the focus of that much attention. "Well, it hasn't happened yet," she said. "Mercury might just stop short and dig his toes in again." Then she smiled. "But he does love an audience, so you never know."

Mercury seemed to sense that today was somehow different as Amy led him out onto the yard and down to the training ring. He jogged and arched his neck proudly.

"OK, boy," laughed Amy. "You're going to get your chance to show off in a minute."

But first, she joined up with him again, using a fence across the ring that was the highest she'd used yet. Mercury sailed over, then followed her devotedly around the ring. She turned and patted him in delight as Bill jumped into the ring to set up two of the jumps at an easy distance from each other. Amy led Mercury to the fence, where she'd balanced his saddle. She placed it on his back and did up the girth, then mounted.

"You can do it, boy," she murmured, turning him back into the ring.

Rather than riding straight at the jumps, Amy trotted Mercury in some neat circles and figure eights, then slowed him to a walk and rode over to the first of the jumps. "What do you think, boy?" she asked, letting him stretch out his neck and sniff the jump. "Want to try it?"

Mercury showed no signs of his earlier wariness, so Amy rode him to the second jump and let him sniff that, too. Then she trotted him away and turned him in a large circle before nudging him into a canter. She turned him toward the first jump, her heart pounding as they drew nearer. Her whole body was braced for a refusal. But Mercury's ears pricked forward, and she felt the eagerness and power of his muscles. One, two strides, and they were up and over. Amy heard a burst of applause, and a grin stretched right across her face.

"Now the second one," she whispered to Mercury. She collected him slightly, then turned his head to the jump. Mercury snorted, then bounded forward. "Steady," cautioned Amy. He shortened his stride and then, again, they were over, with a good foot to spare.

"Mercury! You're amazing!" Amy cried, clapping him on the neck.

Mercury pranced on the spot and arched his neck, as if to say *I know*. Amy laughed and looked over at the fence, where the whole Whitepath family was watching her. She rode over and dismounted, unable to stop grinning. For once, Huten's inscrutable face broke into a big smile.

"He'll go far," he murmured, stroking Mercury's nose. "He's a horse that likes to shine."

Amy couldn't agree more.

❧

The branch of a beech tree tapped gently against the cabin window as Amy and Huten had a final cup of coffee together on Saturday morning. Amy was waiting for Ty to arrive with the trailer to pick up her and Mercury. She was taking the chance to talk to Huten for the last time.

Cradling his coffee mug in his hands, Huten regarded her with a serious expression.

"Thank you for coming," he said gravely. "It took courage."

Amy flushed slightly. "To be honest," she confessed in a low voice, "it felt more like I was escaping something. But I'm glad I came. Very glad."

Huten nodded slowly. "Follow your instincts," he said. "Just as your mother learned to do."

"Is that what she learned here?" asked Amy tentatively.

Huten smiled. "When she came, she wanted clear answers about her life," he said. "Yes and no. Right and wrong. Whether things would work out. Here, she learned to let life reveal itself in its own way. I think that this is what you have learned, too — that thinking too much about a result can get in the way. That every new day brings its own lessons."

"Yes," agreed Amy quietly. "And I'm going to take things a step at a time from now on. And step back and look at things differently, when I need to."

Huten smiled. "You have also done something very precious. You have fulfilled your mother's promise," he said. "I understand why she never came. Life has a habit of imposing restrictions upon us. And it can also be easy to see death in that way. But in coming here, you have freed it of its restrictions."

Amy struggled to understand his words. He stared into his coffee and murmured, "One of my forebears once said, 'There is no death, only a change of worlds.' Remember that. It might be of comfort to you."

Amy felt a lump in her throat at his reference to Marion's death. She swallowed and nodded. "It will," she whispered.

She heard the rattle of a trailer outside in the driveway and stood up. "Thank you for everything," she said to Huten. "I'm sure this isn't a final good-bye."

"I know it isn't." He smiled.

Amy rushed out of the cabin to greet Ty, who was just climbing out of the trailer. Her heart leaped wildly at the sight of his tall form and familiar dark hair flopping over his forehead.

"Ty!" she cried.

He grinned and held out his arms. Amy fell into them, laughing. She didn't care that Bill and Barbara were already on the yard, watching as Ty bent down to kiss her. She was just so glad to see him.

"I missed you," he said.

"Me, too — it feels like I haven't seen you for a

month, not a week," she said, looking around at the smiling faces in front of her. Carey had brought Mercury out of his stall. Ty let go of Amy and went around to the back of the trailer to undo the bolts. Carey held on to Mercury while Amy quickly secured the travel wraps.

"There," she said when she'd finished. She smiled up at Carey.

"He's all yours," said Carey, smiling back. But Amy could see a wistful look in her eyes, and impulsively she stepped forward to hug the other girl.

"It's been great meeting you, Carey," she said. "Good luck with everything."

"You, too," said Carey. "I'll miss you. But I won't forget you. I hope you come back — soon."

"Maybe you could come to Heartland?" suggested Amy.

"I'd like that," agreed Carey, her face lighting up.

Amy shook hands with Barbara and Bill, then turned toward Huten.

"Good-bye, Huten," she said.

Huten stepped forward and took both her hands. "Good-bye, Amy," he said. "Have a good trip back."

Amy nodded and smiled. She looked around. "It's been a really special week," she said. "I'll never forget it. Thank you."

❧

Amy and Ty climbed into the truck and Ty started the engine. As they drove slowly out of the yard, Amy waved, smiling as Carey slowly raised her arm.

"It's been an amazing week, Ty," she said when they were out on the road. "But I can't wait to see Heartland again. I've missed you all so much. You've got to tell me everything. About everyone. And all the horses."

"Well, that should fill most of the trip," laughed Ty. "But I'm more interested in hearing about your week."

"OK, we'll take turns," said Amy, grinning at him. "But you go first." She frowned, remembering the difficult times before she left. "How's Ben doing?"

"He's been taking it really slowly with Red," said Ty. "He went back to basics, and he's just building him up again. He decided to skip his next show."

"Really?" Amy was astonished. Ben was about to move up from High Prelim, and missing out on a show might set him back.

"Yeah. He's fine about it, though," Ty assured her. "He says he thinks a setback can teach you more, in the long run."

"Yes," said Amy, thinking of how much she had learned from all that had happened. "I guess it can."

They drove in silence for a few minutes. Then Ty turned to her. "Come on, your turn," he said. "Tell me more about your week."

Amy looked at Ty. There was something she was still puzzling over. *"Only a change of worlds,"* she said slowly. *"There is no death, only a change of worlds.* That's what Huten said to me before I left."

Ty frowned. "What do you think he meant?" he asked.

"He was talking about Mom," Amy said in a low voice. She looked out the window for a while. "I think he meant that her spirit will never die," she said eventually. "That it may have changed, but it lives on. In us. In me."

Ty nodded. "I can see that," he said softly. "I can see Marion's spirit in you, all the time."

Amy's eyes filled with tears, but they were tears of happiness. As they drew nearer to Heartland, she realized that some things always remained the same. The spirit of love that had made Heartland home; the spirit of horses that overcame their fears. Other things changed and would continue to change, and that was how it should be. But throughout everything that lay ahead was the spirit of hope — the hope for a bright future, with every new day.

*Share the Moments with Amy
in the next* Heartland *title:*

Tomorrow's Promise

Amy raced to the main entrance of the show grounds just in time to see her boyfriend, Ty, pulling his pickup into the lot. Seeing his familiar face scanning the crowd for her, Amy felt a quiet happiness well up inside. For years, Ty had been just like an older brother working at Heartland farm with her, but a few months ago they had started dating. It had been difficult at first — dealing with becoming more than friends. But things were going well now, and Amy was certain that their relationship had never been better.

She jogged over to the truck. "Hi!" she said, scrambling onto the bench seat. "I've had the best day. Hannah and Gerry looked great — they won the Children's Jumper Classic — and I saw Nick Halliwell — he said he might have a horse to send to us. And the Six-Bar class was amazing. You wouldn't have believed it. There was this strawberry roan mare. She —"

"Amy," Ty interrupted her.

Amy suddenly realized that Ty hadn't reacted to a word she'd said.

"What's up?" she asked in surprise. "Is something wrong?"

"Amy, you've had a phone call . . . from your father."

❧

"A horse?" Amy said to Ty in disbelief. "What do you mean he's bought us a horse?" Her mind was spinning. Was this for real? "You looked so serious. I thought something awful had happened."

Amy could hardly believe it. Until a visit a few months ago, Amy and her sister, Lou, hadn't talked to their father for twelve years. Now Ty was saying that the same man who had once abandoned them had bought them a horse, and that it was arriving that afternoon. "Tell me everything," she said excitedly.

"All I know is it's sixteen hands and a Warmblood gelding," Ty told her, turning the pickup out of the show grounds. "Your dad just called a few hours ago. Lou and your grandpa were out so I talked to him. He said he's been over here on business. He was looking for young horses to export to Australia, and when he saw this horse he decided to buy it for you and Lou."

"But why?" Amy burst out. "Did he say?"

"No, he didn't say anything else." Ty answered. "He was heading out to see someone and couldn't talk long. He's going to call again tonight."

Amy sank back in the seat. She and Lou were getting a horse. A horse that wouldn't have to be rehomed or go back to its owners like most of the other horses at Heartland. Excitement surged through her, but at the same time, she couldn't help wondering why their dad had bought them a horse. After all, it wasn't as if they needed another horse at Heartland. She already had Sundance, and Lou was scared of riding — she had been for twelve years, ever since the riding accident that had ended their father's show-jumping career.

A thought struck Amy as she remembered how, during their father's recent visit, Lou had promised him that she would try to face her fear and start riding again. Maybe he had bought this horse for Lou. Their father was an experienced horseman. It was his business to match horses with riders. He must have realized that they didn't have many horses at Heartland that would be reliable enough for a nervous rider. *Of course*, Amy thought. *That's it. It makes sense.*

"You're awfully quiet," Ty said, looking at her curiously.

"I've just been thinking about why Daddy bought us this horse," Amy answered. "I think it's for Lou. He found a reliable, quiet horse that she can trust, so she can get her confidence back."

"Could be," Ty said thoughtfully.

"I bet I'm right," Amy said, convinced. "I can't wait till it gets here. I wonder what it's like. How old? What color?" A grin spread across her face. What did the details matter? It was a horse of their own — and it was coming to Heartland that afternoon. What could be better than that?

WIN A Horse Lover's Kit!

Enter the *I Love Horses Sweepstakes* and you could win one of 50 Horse Lover's Kits (Est. Ret. Val. $15.00). See sweepstakes rules below.

Name: _____

Address: _____

City: _____ State: _____ Zip: _____

Phone: _____ Birthdate: _____

OFFICIAL RULES (available upon request)

NO PURCHASE NECESSARY. To enter, fill out the coupon above, download an entry form at www.scholastic.com/contests or print your name, complete address (including city, state, and zip code), home phone number, and birthdate on a postcard or a 3-inch-by-5-inch card or sheet of paper, and mail it to I Love Horses, Trade Marketing, 557 Broadway, New York, NY 10012-3999. All entries must be received by October 31, 2002. All winners will be selected by a random drawing. Winners will be notified by November 21, 2002. Scholastic is not responsible for late, lost, stolen, misdirected, damaged, mutilated, postage due, incomplete, or illegible entries or mail.

Sweepstakes is open to residents of the United States who are 14 years or younger as of December 31, 2002. Employees, and members of their families living in the same household, of Scholastic Inc., its parent, subsidiaries, brokers, distributors, dealers, retailers, affiliates, and their respective advertising, promotion and production agencies, are not eligible to enter. Void where prohibited by law.

One entry per person. Winners' first names, states, and ages may be posted on www.scholastic.com/kids/games.htm. Fifty (50) winners will receive a Horse Lover's Kit with a horse charm, journal, stationery, pens, and rubber stamps (estimated retail value of $15.00). All prizes will be awarded. Odds of winning depend on number of entries. All entrants, as a condition of entry, agree to release Scholastic Inc., its affiliates, subsidiaries, distributors, and agencies from any and all liability for injuries or damages of any kind sustained through participation in this sweepstakes and/or use of a prize once accepted.

No cash substitutions, transfers, or assignments of prizes allowed, except by Scholastic in case of unavailability, in which case a prize of equal or greater value will be awarded.

Each winner will be required to sign and return an affidavit of eligibility and liability/publicity release within fifteen days of notification attempt or an alternate winner may be selected. By accepting the prize, each winner grants to Scholastic the right to use his or her name, likeness, hometown, biographical information, and entry for purposes of advertising and promotion without further notice or compensation, except where prohibited by law. Taxes on prizes are the sole responsibility of the prize winners and their families.

For the names of the prize winners (available after November 21, 2002), send a self-addressed stamped envelope to: *I Love Horses Winner's List*, Trade Marketing, 557 Broadway, New York, NY 10012-3999.

Sponsor: Scholastic Inc., 557 Broadway, New York, NY 10012